TIGHT Hold

LISA SUZANNE

TIGHT HOLD
VEGAS ACES: THE TIGHT END
BOOK TWO
© 2022 Lisa Suzanne

Published in the United States of America by Books by LS, LLC.

ISBN: 9798422976423

This book is a work of fiction. Any similarities to real people, living or dead, is purely coincidental. All characters and events in this work are figments of the author's imagination.

BOOKS BY LISA SUZANNE

VEGAS ACES
Home Game (Book One)
Long Game (Book Two)
Fair Game (Book Three)
Waiting Game (Book Four)
End Game (Book Five)

VEGAS ACES: THE QUARTERBACK
Traded (Book One)
Tackled (Book Two)
Timeout (Book Three)
Turnover (Book Four)
Touchdown (Book Five)

A LITTLE LIKE DESTINY SERIES
A Little Like Destiny (Book One)
Only Ever You (Book Two)
Clean Break (Book Three)

MY FAVORITE BAND STANDALONES
Take My Heart
The Benefits of Bad Decisions
Waking Up Married
Driving Me Crazy
It's Only Temporary
The Replacement War

Visit Lisa on Amazon for more titles

DEDICATION

To my favorite 3Ms.

CHAPTER 1

Ben

Kaylee's eyes are wide, but I maintain my cool as always.

An important lesson I learned over the last decade playing professional football—and maybe even before that, really, as I faced many different types of opponents—is that you never let the enemy see you sweat.

And in this case, Shannon with the crazy eyes is the enemy. Who the fuck walks into a room and just blackmails everybody in it?

"Listen, Shannon," I say, using the low pitch of my voice to try to reason with her despite the lessons of my past that prove you can't reason with crazy. "For starters, I'm sorry you're going through a hard time. Truly. My parents divorced when I was young, and it was pretty much enough to turn me off to marriage for the rest of my life. But beyond that, I saw your shadow in your bedroom just before I walked into Kaylee's room. I gave her the signal to follow my lead, and *that* is what you overheard. The only thing we're faking is the conversation you so conveniently recorded, and it was all just a joke for your benefit."

She shrugs. "Doesn't matter. Those celebrity gossip bloggers will have a field day with this recording."

"They won't give a shit about it, and just for your future reference, blackmail is in fact illegal," I say. I keep my tone flippant even though I'm secretly fucking outraged that this bitch could blow everything up before we've even gone out on our first date. Clearly we need to be more careful, but I thought we were safe in Jack's house with the usual residents downstairs engaging with their children. "You want me to prove that we're not faking a relationship?"

Shannon's crazy eyes dart between Kaylee and me, and that's when I saunter over to Kaylee's bed, climb on it, and kick a leg over so I'm hovering over her.

Her breathing quickens, and as my eyes bore down into hers, I see the panic there. I try to soothe that panic with my own look of confidence. I lower my lips to hers, and she wraps her arms around my neck as she deepens the kiss.

It takes all of a few milliseconds for my body to respond, but before I allow myself to get into it, I pull back and turn toward Shannon. "Proof enough for you?"

She shakes her head. "Not until I see you do that in front of everyone downstairs."

I roll my eyes. "We have nothing to prove to you. Do whatever you want with that recording. I won't be blackmailed over a joke." I glance away from her and give Kaylee the look that I pray tells her to just go along with me. "Kay, you ready?"

She nods, and I climb off her and hold out a hand to help her up. Together we brush past Shannon and head downstairs. I keep my fingers linked with hers as we enter the room where Jack and Luke are hanging with their wives and kids, and Jack glances up at us first.

I throw my head quickly toward Shannon, who followed closely behind us down the stairs, and then I toss an arm around Kaylee's shoulders and squeeze her to my side. She links an arm around my waist, and as odd as it is doing this in front of her entire family, it still feels so completely right.

"How's the happy new couple?" Jack asks, and thank God he read my signal correctly. I guess that's what happens after you've played on a team with a guy for a few years. You learn to read each other's signals even off the field.

I lean down and press my lips to Kaylee's temple. "Great," I say.

There's an awkward beat of silence, and I fill it. "Shannon is accusing us of faking it after we put on a little act for her benefit." I let out a chuckle.

Shannon's eyes widen as I tell on her.

Kate, who looks some combination of angry and confused, speaks up first. "She accused you of faking what? Your relationship?"

I nod.

Kate huffs out a laugh. "Right. Have you seen these two lovebirds?" she asks Shannon. "They're all over each other all the time." She rolls her eyes like it's so gross, and Jack, Ellie, and Luke all nod in agreement.

"I can't help it," I say, reaching down to squeeze her ass. "She's hot as fuck."

Kaylee yelps a little at the pinch I give her, Jack's vein is starting to bulge again, Luke looks like he's going to be sick, and Kate and Ellie both give me the same look of warning for swearing in front of their kids.

Kaylee reaches up onto her tiptoes and presses a kiss to my mouth. "Right back at you, Big O." She wiggles her eyebrows, and I laugh. "He's *really* proven how he earned that nickname."

We're riding a fine line here between putting on an act and telling the truth.

"Why would you accuse them of faking it?" Kate asks Shannon.

"I just, you know…" Shannon says, trying to backpedal. "I overheard them talking and they were making it sound like

9

they're putting on some act for the media and also how Kaylee hasn't had to fake—"

I interrupt her before she gets to the part about Kaylee and me actually fucking. "She recorded our conversation. I saw her before I turned into Kaylee's room, so we put on a little show for her. Then she came in and tried to blackmail me."

Kate stands. "She tried to what?" Her voice is a low hiss, and holy hell, she's up there among the kindest women I've ever met, but you also don't want to get on her bad side. "Shannon, are you kidding me? After what you did to me, I tried to be kind. I let you stay longer even though you said it would only be one night and even though Jack didn't want you here…and then you try to blackmail my family?"

Shannon's crazy eyes go wide. "I…uh…oh, I—I just thought that maybe Ben could play *my* boyfriend just to get back at Kevin a little for the things he's been doing." The waterworks start, but unfortunately, not a soul in this room buys it or cares.

"Get the hell out of my house," Kate seethes. "Now. Lose my number. Lose this address. You just killed any sort of hope for a reconciliation between the two of us. Our friendship was over before, but I gave you a second chance. You can forget that now."

Jack stands. "Before you go, could you be so kind as to delete that illegal voice recording? Like right now so we can all watch as you delete it?"

Shannon is still crying, but she brought this on herself. She pulls her phone out of her pocket as she swipes away a tear, and then she looks between Kaylee and me. "I'm sorry." Her apology holds little weight. She pulls open her voice memos and deletes the most recent one.

"Delete it out of your deleted folder, too," I say so she can't go recover it in secret later and figure out some way to use it against me. I lean over and take a look at what she's doing.

"Ooh, good call," Kaylee says.

"Not my first blackmail rodeo," I say with a wink, and Kaylee laughs. "Play the most recent one," I say just to make *totally* sure she deleted the one of our conversation.

Her shoulders sag as she plays it, and we all hear Jack's voice. The one before that is Jack and Luke, and then one of Kate talking to JJ, and more of Jack.

"You came here to spy on us?" Kate asks, and now her eyes are filling with unshed tears as the betrayal hits her.

Shannon presses her lips together then blows out a breath. "I…I'm sorry. Michelle and Savannah paid us a lot of money before, and I just thought if I could find something—"

Jack snorts, cutting her off. "Michelle's undergoing psychotherapy and Savannah no longer has a job, so I doubt either of them are planning to have you on their payroll anytime soon."

Shannon glances around at the eyes on her. "It was wrong. I know that. You've all been so kind to me the last few days, and I'm so sorry. I've hit rock bottom…" She turns her gaze down to the ground. "It's not an excuse for what I've done. I'll just go get my things and be on my way."

"Uh, that's funny, but you get the fuck out of my house now," Jack says, sauntering over from his spot in the family room. He holds his hand out. "Give me your phone since it's evidence now. Leave your shit upstairs because fuck you if you think you're going to steal from me. I will send it along when I feel like it."

Shannon's mouth drops open. "I didn't steal anything!"

Jack's brows rise, and he looks like he's barely hanging onto his composure. "You stole my wife's trust. Now hand over the goddamn phone before I call the police."

"You can't just take my phone," she says.

"Watch me." He reaches over and grabs it out of her hand. "You can't just do what you did and expect to get away with it. You betrayed my wife, my child, my siblings, my best friend, my family, and myself. You fucked with the wrong people. Now fuck off out of here."

"I need my keys," she says flatly, clearly holding back her tears.

"Where are they?" Kaylee asks.

"My dresser."

"Not *your* dresser. The dresser in the room you overstayed your welcome in," Jack corrects.

Kaylee runs upstairs and retrieves the keys, and then Jack walks her to the front door and slams it behind her while Ellie hugs a trembling Kate.

"I was so stupid to trust her," Kate says when Jack walks back into the room.

"You're kind and forgiving, Kia," he says, using his nickname for her. He wraps his arms around her as Ellie lets her go. "You weren't stupid. You were wonderful, and she didn't deserve it."

"I'm sorry I let her back in." Her voice is muffled as she cries into his chest.

"She's gone now," Jack says, soothing his wife. "And I'll be calling Richard to see if we can press any charges."

It's such an odd thing to see this beast of a quarterback show his tender side, but Kate and JJ do that to him. It's incredible, really.

And I can't help but wonder if that's something I could have, too.

With Kaylee Dalton.

CHAPTER 2

Kaylee

Ben hung around most of the day yesterday after the trauma with Shannon mostly to make sure Jack didn't need anything. Jack spoke with his lawyer and we learned that in Nevada, listening to or recording a conversation without consent is a Category D Felony that carries up to four years in prison or a hefty fine, and Jack is determined to press charges.

There had to be at least twenty private conversations recorded on her phone—none incriminating, but it doesn't matter. It was a breach of privacy for all of us.

Once the kids were down for the night, we spent time sitting around Jack's fire pit drinking beer and roasting marshmallows as the men reminisced about their recent Super Bowl win.

And now I'm nearly ready for our first official date. My hair and make-up are done, and I haven't put this much effort into my appearance in far too long. The daily grind of teaching has weighed heavily on me this year, and I just haven't had the time—or the reason since I haven't gone on a date worth this much effort.

I slip my dress over my head, carefully avoiding my hair and face so as not to mess up the work it took to create perfect beach waves, and then I step into my shoes. I add one final touch of jewelry then glance at myself in the mirror attached to my dresser.

I feel good as I review the dress I chose for our date. It's a strappy black bandage dress with a plunging front and back V-neck that hugs every curve I own. A bit of lace detail around the neckline matches the short sleeves and the hem at the bottom, and while it's revealing, it's also *fancy dinner* appropriate.

And probably the biggest benefit of this particular dress is that Ben is going to be panting all night as he patiently waits to get me home so he can properly work me over.

Or, maybe if the mood strikes, he'll find a time or a place to work me over before we even leave the dinner.

He's picking me up at Jack's place at eight, and I'm ready with only seconds to spare. I hear the doorbell as I make my descent down the stairs. Jack and Kate are outside by the fire pit and JJ's down for the night, so I move toward the door to answer it.

I open it and find a freaking fantasy standing on the other side.

Ben Olson is wearing a suit.

My lips part as a small gasp escapes me. My mouth waters as my eyes flick down his figure.

He's always hot. He's got a great body, which makes sense considering he's a professional athlete. He's tall and lean. When he's walking around in those grey shorts with a hat backwards on his head, he's ridiculously sexy.

But in that suit…holy hell. He's otherworldly. He's perfection.

And, for the next few months, he's *mine*.

"Wow," he murmurs.

My eyes move up to his at his single word.

"You look incredible," he says.

"Thank you," I say softly, words barely forming. "You…uh…"

He glances doubtfully down at his suit. "Does this look okay?"

Ben Olson unsure and vulnerable in a suit. Now *that* is something you don't see every day.

"It looks more than *okay*, Ben. You look real freaking hot."

He chuckles. "As do you, my gorgeous date." He steps in and takes a quick glance around.

"They're outside," I murmur, and he leans down to press a soft kiss to my lips at the all-clear.

I tip my head back and link my arms around his neck as I pull him in a little closer, turning the soft kiss a little rougher, a little more urgent as the sudden need to *show* him what I think about that suit pulses through me.

His hands move to my hips as his tongue batters mine, and any semblance of coherent thought takes a backseat as primal urges and desires take over.

His grip tightens on my hips, and he backs away a little as he leans his forehead down to mine. "Fuck, I want you," he says, and his hips buck toward mine to give me a little taste of what's to come later.

"Right back at you, Trouble," I say, and I nip at his lips once more before I let him go.

"We need to go," he says.

"Yeah." I clear my throat and back out of his fresh scent orbit before I cling back onto him and don't let go. I have a feeling this entire night is going to feel like foreplay, and I'm going to be positively aching for him by the time we finally get to the part of the night I'm craving.

"Let me just say hi to Jack," he says.

I nod, and we walk through the house toward the backyard.

"The Big O and my little sister," Jack says. His eyes fall to me, and I spot a bit of disapproval for my dress of choice. So it's a *little* revealing. I'm also twenty-two and don't mind showing off my assets, and he needs to remember he's my *brother*. Lately it seems like he's trying to step into the role of our dad, and it's just another reminder that dad's gone and it's time for me to move out of my brother's place. "Take care of her and keep your hands to yourself."

Thankfully he doesn't mention the dress, and Kate grins. "Have fun, kids," she says playfully, and then we're on our way.

We take the car waiting out front for us arranged by Ben toward Las Vegas Boulevard and turn toward a few popular hotels located off-Strip. We pull in front of a large, two-story building with a splashy sign out front reading *West End Lounge*, likely because it's located west of the main drag where many major hotels and casinos are located in Vegas. A red carpet is set up out front with bright lights pointed at a backdrop of the West End Lounge logo, and a stream of photographers wait on either side of the red carpet.

"Ready for our first official appearance together?" Ben asks as we both look at the red carpet.

I blow out a breath. "No turning back now, right?"

He leans in and presses a soft kiss to my mouth. "You can always back out, Peaches."

"What if I don't want to?"

He pulls back just slightly and studies my eyes for a beat. "I don't want you to."

My chest tightens at his words.

Neither of us is backing out. Neither of us wants to.

But neither of us wants a serious relationship, either.

I respond with another soft kiss to his lips, and then he opens the door. He helps me out, and a few flashbulbs go off in our faces as the photographers each angle for a glimpse of who superstar Ben Olson brought as his date tonight.

"Olson, who's the mystery woman?" one of the photographers yells.

Ben just nods politely and doesn't say anything, which means he's going to make it somebody's homework to figure out who I am.

"Olson, over here!" someone else yells.

More questions are fired at us, and we just smile and move along the carpet toward the backdrop to get our photos taken there. Ben's hand clasps mine firmly as we walk, and he tosses an arm around my shoulders and pulls me in close once we're at the backdrop.

"Now one with just Olson!" someone yells, and Ben ignores them, tightening his grip around me.

He looks at me and nods, the signal that we're done with the photos, and a hostess standing off to the side ushers us into the club.

I immediately spot Andrew Kinney, the actor who hit on me at Ben's pool party not so long ago. I spot a few players from the Aces, some hockey players from the local team, a few other celebrities who look familiar, and, to my total excitement that awakens the fangirl inside me, two members of Vail, one of my favorite bands. In total, I'd estimate around twenty-five celebrities here plus their dates, and it's like a *Who's Who* of Vegas-based celebrities.

Ben seems to know everyone, which is no surprise, and he just introduces me as his date Kaylee. No last names. No *girlfriend* talk. Yet. It is, after all, our first public appearance, and while nobody knows how long we've been dating behind closed doors, we still have a certain perception we need to give. I stay close by his side, and he keeps his arm wrapped around me.

I can just see the headlines now. *Aces Star Tight End Getting Cozy with Mystery Woman.*

That's me. I'm the mystery woman.

And the more time I spend with Ben, the more excited I am about this entire plan.

CHAPTER 3

Ben

The drinks are flowing, and I can't stop smelling her hair. Is that her shampoo? Is it some spray she uses? Perfume? Or is that sunshine smell just *her*?

It's strange, really, how a scent can just call to me and awaken parts of me that've been dormant for over a decade.

A wall of flowers with a neon sign in the center proclaiming the word *love* has everybody stopping for a photo op before we sit down to dinner.

We're not there. We won't *go* there, either. I can't.

Just *seeing* the word there makes me sweat uncomfortably.

But the word is out there now, mingling between the two of us as we make the rounds. We finally head toward our table. Each couple has their own table for two that faces the front of the room so we can get a view of what it would be like to eat here when the club is actually open.

The other three Aces players I've spotted since we walked into the place—Jaxon Bryant, Eric Scott, and Patrick Harris, each with a date—are all spread out across the room. Instead of seating us near people we know, we're located in the back. In front of us are a local news anchor, a drummer from a well-known band, and an *influencer* who apparently got her start on a reality show.

"Oh my God," Kaylee whispers. I glance over at her. Her eyes are on the drummer. "It's Ethan Fuller from Vail! So close to our table!"

I glance at the woman sitting beside him. "With his wife," I point out, and Kaylee rolls her eyes. "And you're here with a date, too, remember?"

She giggles. "Are you *jealous*, Mr. Olson?"

"Nah." I shake my head. "That guy's probably jealous of *me*."

She raises a brow. "Because you play football?"

I give her the smoothest answer ever. "Nope. Because I've got the hottest date in the place."

She giggles and smacks me in the chest, and we sit. As usual at these types of events, someone at the front of the room starts talking shortly after we sit. We're thanked for our time and encouraged to have fun, and then the first course is served as the music turns up and we're treated to a show of dancers in the Cirque du Soleil style.

Kaylee nods toward the *love* wall. "You ever been in love?" she asks. We can have our own private conversation over the music without risking anyone around us overhearing, particularly here in the back of the room where we sit and watch the dancers.

"Starting deep for our first date, Peaches." I brush it off mostly because I don't really want to get into it.

She shrugs. "Just making conversation and getting to know the guy I'm dating a little better."

"Once. You?"

She nods. "Same."

"What ended it?" I ask.

"He didn't want the same future I wanted. You?"

I nod. "Same."

"How long ago was yours?" She plays with the goat cheese walnut thing on her plate and keeps her eyes on the dancers.

As for me, I don't eat anything that was squeezed out of a goat, so I play around with the nuts a little. The ones on my plate, I mean. For now, anyway. "A decade," I admit. "You?"

"My senior year of college."

"Isn't that a little early to be figuring out what you want for your future?" I ask.

She lifts a shoulder and glances up at me. The way her eyelashes are sort of lowered and she peeks up at me through them is so goddamn sexy that I want to shove her up against the *love* wall and show her a real nice time. Or any other wall. It doesn't have to be the *love* one.

She shakes her head. "There are just some things you *know* from the beginning of time, right? And I've always known I wanted to be a wife and a mother. I want a whole bunch of kids and I want to support all their different interests. I want a dog, maybe some chickens, maybe a horse or two. I want to live on a huge plot of land with nothing around us for miles, maybe with some paths so I can run at dawn and hike with the kids during the day. I want peace and quiet and privacy since my entire family has been the center of attention since I was a pre-teen. I want open sky and cool air blowing in the windows. And if you know where such a place exists, please take me there."

My stomach twists in a knot. Oh, I know a place *exactly* like the one she just described.

Complete with chickens and horses, if she's really so inclined, and a dog named Buddy who's scared of spiders.

The only thing it doesn't come with is the husband who wants kids, too.

She keeps babbling as if she didn't just turn my entire world upside down. "I've always seen my future that way, but the face of the man has been blank, ready to be filled in with the perfect man. Dane was a city boy through and through. He thinks dogs are dirty and he doesn't really like kids. He never would've liked the peaceful, quiet dream of a home filled with kids and pets I've wanted since I was six-years-old and saw the perfect place on some soap opera my mom was watching. In fact, he moved to Chicago to start a job at Morgan Stanley after we graduated, and now he lives in some skyscraper in the heart of downtown." She shrugs as she finishes her tirade, but I'm still stuck back a minute ago when she described my place in Montana almost to an exact T.

"I was traded from Chicago when the Aces acquired me," I say stupidly rather than responding to anything else she said, my eyes still on the dancers.

She nods. "Did you like it there?"

It feels like a trap. If I say yes, does that mean she's going to go back and try to be with her ex? It's only been a year since she broke it off with him. I blow out a breath. I'm not used to weighing my words like this. "It's a great city full of great people, but it never felt like home."

"Is it weird feeling like every city you live in is temporary?" She sets her fork down, giving up on the goat cheese walnut thing.

I lift a shoulder. "Sort of feels normal after all this time, but I admit it would be nice to figure out where I eventually want to settle."

"Not Montana?" she presses.

"Maybe Montana, though it's a little close to my ex and my mother."

"Tell me about them," she says. She picks up her glass to take a sip of her wine, and I set my fork down, too.

We still have another few minutes *at least* until anyone's coming by to pick up our plates and deliver the next course, and I have something way more interesting to fill the time than discussing the women who have destroyed my faith in love.

"I could do that," I say quietly, and I slide a hand along her leg. I reach toward her inner thigh and brush my fingers against the soft edge of her panties. "Or I could do this."

She sets her glass down as her legs fall open for me. Her lips part and her breathing quickens, and *fuck* she's pretty like this when she's all hot and ready for me.

I slip the panties over with my finger, and she widens her legs just a little more. I keep my eyes on her profile as she stares straight ahead wordlessly.

"You want to tell me more about *Of Mice and Men*?" I croon close to her ear as I slide a finger through her slit and massage her clit for a beat.

"Mm," is her first reply, followed by a moaned, "God, you're trouble."

I chuckle as I move my finger down and find the promised land. Even though she's wet as fuck, it's still a tight fit as I push a finger inside, and she shifts a little in her chair. "You already knew that."

She glances over at me, her eyes full of need and lust when they connect with mine. "Yeah, I did. And I'm starting to like it more and more."

My finger continues to thrust while she talks, and her eyes are glazed as I move my finger in and out of her body. I slip it out and massage her clit again, and that's when she grips onto the edge of the table. She keeps her eyes on the dancers, but I only have eyes for her. I feel her legs tighten against my hand as they clench together, and I watch her face as she falls apart from my touch. She's trying to keep her eyes open, trying to focus on the dancers, trying to maintain that we're cool back here, and she snags her bottom lip between her teeth as she can't take it anymore. Her hand grips onto my wrist, her nails digging into my skin, and her eyes close as she tips her head back. I'm treated to a quiet moan that'll replay in my dreams tonight as she comes as quietly as she can beside me.

When the clenching of her thighs loosens, I pull my hand back. She glances over at me a little lazily, like she could take a nap after what I just did to her, and *Jesus* she's hot.

"All that before the second course," she says.

I lean in close to her ear and press a soft kiss to her neck. "I want you to be the third course."

She shivers a little then tips her head back and leans toward me for a soft kiss. "Maybe a second dessert back at your place."

I chuckle as I toss an arm around her shoulders. "You don't want to meet me in the bathroom and suck my cock?"

Her eyes widen a little and her jaw slackens. "Apart from the bathroom part of that proposition, yeah, I actually really do want to do that."

I laugh. "We've got all night, babe. If you want somewhere a little nicer than a club bathroom, I'll wait. Though if we're really testing out the features of this club, we should probably at least give it a try."

She narrows her eyes at me. "You do that in club bathrooms often?"

I shrug. "Depends on your definition of *often*."

She makes a face like she just smelled something bad. "Gross."

"But now that I've got a girlfriend, it'll only be with you."

She laughs. "I'm not sure that makes it any better."

The waitress swings by to take the goat food away and drop off our second course, some sort of butternut soup, and Kaylee is relaxed and smiling.

The wicked side of me says that's the way I plan to keep her for the next few months until our deal is over.

And then she can move on with her life. She can find that husband who wants a litter of kids with her because she deserves everything she wants out of life.

Part of me wishes I could be the one to give all that to her, but deep down, I know I can't. She started asking the questions, so maybe it's time I give her the answers. That way I can fend off any potential questions about where this might go next since whatever fun we're having together is all this can ever be.

CHAPTER 4

Kaylee

We're somewhere around the fifth course—I think—when Ben takes a bite of the fish and wrinkles his nose.

To be honest, I've lost count of which course we're on and all this food is weird anyway. I'm hungry and I just want a juicy burger and fries, though typically that's not really on my diet. I'm more of a grilled chicken and veggies kind of girl.

He takes another bite of the fish then sets his fork down. "You wanna get the fuck out of here and grab a burger somewhere?"

It's like he can read my mind.

I giggle. "I thought you'd never ask."

We stand and head toward the exit. We thank the hostess for a nice evening but explain that we have another place to be, and then we walk hand-in-hand out to the car waiting for us.

"In N Out Burger drive-thru," Ben tells our driver, and we're quiet in the backseat for a few beats when he says out of the blue, "Her name was Tatum."

I glance over at him with my brows knit together in question.

"The one woman I loved. Or at least I *thought* I loved."

Oh my God, he's actually opening up. I nod in encouragement for him to go on.

"You gave me a piece of your puzzle, and I want to give you a piece of mine. I wanted to do it back in there, but I didn't want to taint our good time with my history."

He pauses and looks out the window, and he keeps his gaze focused there while he talks. "She moved to Great Falls in the middle of my junior year of high school. She was a year younger than me, but we were in the same math class. I was living with my dad because my mom's house was a revolving door of new men, and I invited her over after school. I was her first. She wasn't mine." His tone is flat as he talks.

He sighs, and I reach over and grab his hand. He keeps talking, his gaze moving down to where our hands our joined. "My entire life was football, but I let her in, too. I didn't have a lot of time between maintaining my C average and practices or workouts. I chose to sign with the University of Montana, three hours from Great Falls, but we decided to stay together. She had a car and came up for every home game, and I thought she was it for me. It was so easy, and while a part of me felt like I was missing out on my college experience, I thought she was worth it. Even though my parents' divorce had turned me off to ever wanting marriage, she made me believe it could work. I bought a ring even though we were too young. We'd been together four years when I was drafted in the first round by the Chargers." He glances out the window.

I'm staring at his profile, and his jaw clenches.

"So what happened?" I ask.

He finally turns to look at me. I see the emotion still there despite all the time that has passed. For as emotionless as he kept his tone, he can't hide it from his eyes.

We turn into the parking lot for the burger joint. There are a few cars ahead of us in the drive-thru line.

He presses his lips together and shrugs. "Things I'm not ready to get into...but suffice it to say she'd been fucking

30

someone else." He shakes his head and closes his eyes. "God, I was a fucking idiot. College should've been parties and experimentation and fun, and instead I was tied to her."

It's clearly one of his life's greatest regrets, and now I see why he developed the reputation of the league's greatest party boy. He missed that stage of life most people experience in college.

"You weren't a fucking idiot," I say softly. He glances over at me. "She was." I want to add more—that she gave up a great guy, and who would do that? But even as I'm about to question it, I realize I'm sort of in the same category.

I don't want the life that goes with being married to a professional athlete. It's been a part of my life for as long as I can remember, forced on me since I was just a twinkle in my dad's eye.

Interestingly, though, Ben's been playing a decade now. His playing career won't last too many more years, and the more time I spend with him, the more I can see him in filling that role of the man in my dreams that never had a face. The fuzziness is starting to clear as I can imagine a future with him in it.

"Thanks for saying that," he says. "My mother killed my trust in women when I found out she'd been stepping out on my dad, and Tatum murdered what little I had left. It's why I decided commitment just isn't for me. I was taught from a young age that women cheat, and so I've built a wall of protection. They're both still back in Montana, and they're basically best friends these days. It's a strange dynamic and it keeps me the hell out of Great Falls."

"Not all women cheat," I say softly. I want to dig more into the *commitment just isn't for me* comment, but I let it go. For now. "Where's your house located? Great Falls?"

He shakes his head. "About an hour and a half southwest of there. Far enough to stay away from both of them, but word travels pretty quickly when I'm in town."

"Seems like there aren't many places you can just go to get away from everything," I muse.

"I've brought a lot of that on myself, though. I stepped into a certain role and built a brand on it, and now it's just what people expect from me."

"Is that what you want out of life?" I ask. I get the feeling from his tone that it isn't. He built a certain reputation maybe to get back at an ex when he was young and in his twenties, but now he's in his thirties and approaching the end of his playing days. Goals and values transition and change as we move through different stages of life, and as an outsider getting to know the person inside, I can't help but wonder if he's living his life based on the world's expectations of how he should live it rather than how he wants to live it.

We're pulling up to the drive-thru speaker now, and he never gets the chance to answer—probably exactly how he wants it. We're getting deep back here, and that wasn't part of the agreement. It wasn't part of the plan.

The car pulls up to the speaker and stops with it right outside Ben's window so he can place the order.

"What do you want?" he asks me.

Well if that isn't a loaded question.

"Just order two of whatever you're having," I say without thinking it through. He's a professional athlete. He can likely put down a few more calories than I should even consider putting down.

"Two double doubles with cheese." He glances at me. "You want a shake?"

I nod. "Chocolate."

"Both with chocolate shakes."

We're quiet while we watch the action inside through a long window. Workers mill about, and the place is busy on a Sunday night. Nobody inside knows that the back of this car holds Aces star tight end Ben Olson and his new fake girlfriend, the sister of Jack and Luke Dalton.

The anonymity is nice, and it's even nicer sharing it in the back of a car with a guy I'm starting to have real feelings for.

CHAPTER 5

Ben

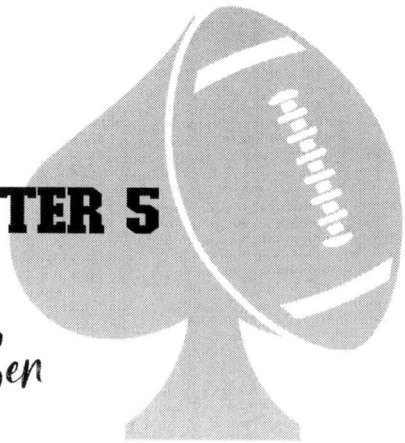

"You still like making silly bets?" she asks once we're back at my place and our spread of food is on the table. She's holding the paper wrapper in her hand and hasn't taken a bite yet while I've already wolfed down half my burger in two bites—and I ditched the wrapper a while ago as she daintily ate one fry at a time.

I raise a brow at her. "How do you know I like making bets?"

She lifts a shoulder. "I don't know. You're around a lot and I guess I pay attention."

I chuckle, and then a little ping of satisfaction darts through my chest as I watch her take her first bite. Her eyes roll back a little as she gives into the deliciousness. "Yeah. I'm always up for a wager amongst friends. You?"

"I was thinking about this Instagram thing and wondering how we could make it a little more…interesting," she says. She takes another bite, and the way she looks like she's in the throes of pleasure as she eats makes my cock twitch. I want to make her pull that same face as I fuck her stupid.

"What are you thinking?"

She shakes her head. "I don't know yet. Maybe something with raising money for the charity we choose."

"I've got an unfair advantage, don't you think?"

Her brows dip. "Because you're a celebrity?"

I nod. "Well, yeah."

"I've got three of those at my disposal. I'll give you your unfair advantage and still beat the pants off you."

I laugh. "Are those the stakes? Because honestly, we don't need a bet for me to drop my pants for you, babe."

She narrows her eyes at me. "No, those are not the stakes."

"Then what are they?"

"Loser plans a mystery date for the winner."

I raise a brow. This could go either way. "All right." I nod. "And how do I win?"

She laughs. "We could keep it simple with whoever raises more money in a given period of time thing."

"How many followers do you have?" I ask.

"I think around a thousand, but my account is private, so I'd need to build it a little first."

"I'm nearing two million. A straight whoever raises the most money competition wouldn't be fair."

She nods and twists her lips as she thinks. "Okay, then let's do something with engagement. Pretend I have a thousand followers and get three hundred likes on a post. That's a thirty percent like rate, and maybe we make comments worth more, so if I get twenty comments, that's a two percent comment rate but we count it as twenty. Average the two and you've got twenty-five for one post. Whoever gets the most engagement over a predetermined period of time once we start this bet wins."

My brows dip in confusion. "That sounds like a lot of math."

"If I'm not working, I could do the math. We could screenshot numbers forty-eight hours after a given post goes up to keep things fair."

"What if I post more than you, or vice versa?" I ask.

"It would obviously be advantageous to post more often, but it's up to you how much you want to do it."

I nod as I squint at her and study her for a beat. "Can I trust you?" I'm being playful even though we just had that serious conversation back in the car about my trust issues.

"Of course you can." Her eyes meet mine, and she sobers for a second. "I'm not like them, Ben," she says softly. "I'd never cheat you out of your victory. I'd never cheat on you *period.*"

Something in her eyes tells me to believe her...but I believed Tatum, too. I believed my mom when she told me the divorce wasn't her fault. I believed everyone who manipulated me before I grew up enough to see them for who they really were.

And now I'm a little older, a little more jaded, and a whole lot more distrustful.

I take a bite of my burger rather than responding, and she does, too.

"Okay, then." I nod. "You've got yourself a deal. When do you want to start?"

"How about when I move in? That gives us a little under a month to figure out a game plan, stockpile photos, for me to start building my account, and to determine our charity. Plus that will give Ellie a head start on finding sponsorships."

"I've given the charity a little more thought," I admit.

"Oh?"

I nod. "When we were talking about it yesterday, I got to thinking about my own gym. Your idea sparked something I've been considering a while. I want to initiate a kids' program. Not a daycare, which is something we already have in place, but something more unique. Something that includes both physical and social development, that promotes physical but also mental health and fitness. We'd build confidence and teamwork and sportsmanship skills through research-based, proven activities, and our charity would allow us to offer scholarships to families who can't afford these types of private programs. I'm thinking something different for every day to keep kids coming back. Sports fundamentals, stretching, boot camp, dance, yoga, martial arts, kickboxing—with a famous football star popping by upon occasion, of course." I flash her a grin. "We could start the program at my gym, make our mistakes, and perfect it before we bring it to a wider community, whether it's gyms all across America, park districts, or something else we come up with."

Her eyes widen with excitement as a smile lights up her whole face. "Oh my God, Ben. I love that idea!"

"Yeah?" I ask, and my smile widens, too.

She nods. "I didn't know you own a gym, but that's the perfect place to create and test the program. And since I have a bit of planning background and a passion for this stuff, could I help with the actual programming?"

"Peaches, you could take it on if you want it," I say, and her excitement is getting me more excited about the idea. "Saves me the hassle of finding someone else to do it."

"Are you kidding me?" she shrieks. "You'd let me take the whole thing on?"

"Absolutely. It's yours. I'll put you in touch with Craig. He's one of my buddies from high school and he runs my gym, and I'm sure he'd be willing to answer any questions you have."

She jumps down from the stool at the pub-style kitchen table this place came with and throws her arms around my neck. "This is *perfect!* It combines my passion for teaching and fitness and kids, and I already have about a zillion ideas."

I chuckle, and I wrap my arms around her. She squeezes me before she pulls back and presses a hard kiss to my mouth, and then her cheeks turn a little pink as she sits back in her chair and picks up her wrapped burger again. Mine's long gone, but I pick up my shake and start sucking it down.

"Now that we have our charity, I really want to beat you," she says. "The more engagement, the more people we're reaching, and the more people we're reaching, the more potential sponsorships and therefore money we can pull in to support this cause."

I narrow my eyes at her. "Like you've got a shot in hell of beating me." It's a clear challenge, and she laughs.

"We'll see."

Indeed we will.

CHAPTER 6

Kaylee

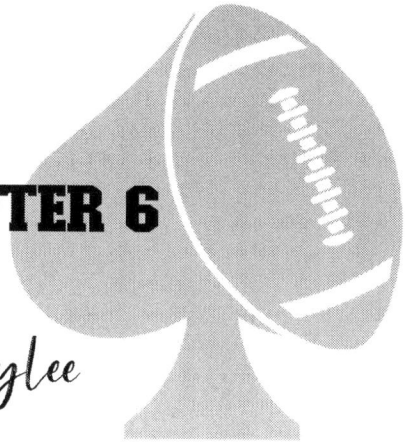

It's Monday morning before school when a text from Ellie comes through.

Ellie: *Wanted you to hear from me first. Can you swing by after school so we can chat out our plan of action? LINK PREVIEW: Billy Peters Latest Celebrity Snaps*

My eyes widen as I read the link preview.

Oh shit.

The first bell rings, which means kids will be filing into my room any second, but I click the link anyway.

"Billy Peters here with your latest Celebrity Snaps!" The popular celebrity gossip vlogger snaps his fingers and a picture from last night's red carpet appears on the screen. Damn, this guy works fast. "First up we have Vegas Aces' tight end Ben Olson with a gorgeous mystery woman on his arm. That alone isn't news since Olson is often spotted with gorgeous women around Vegas, but who's this new lady he's giving his signature Big O Thunder to? Let's take a closer look." The screen zooms in on my face.

"Early reports are telling me that this hot new couple isn't really a couple at all, but the woman in question might be the little sister of the Dalton brothers. Our sources have spotted the Big O coming and going from the very sexy Jack Dalton's

house on many occasions, and all reports indicate Ben and Jack
are besties." He snaps his fingers again, and the words FAKE
NEWS flash across the screen. "A source close to the couple
is claiming they're faking a relationship to help bad boy Ben's
bad boy rep. My people will be digging deeper, so stay tuned.
But for now, let's listen to Ben's Big O Thunder on repeat a
few times and imagine him roaring like that...well, you know."
He snaps and the screen flips to Ben on the field roaring at the
camera.

I don't have to imagine him roaring like that in any other
setting. I've seen it. Naked. And it's hotter than that dumbass
Billy Peters could even imagine.

I draw in a deep breath as I quickly text Ellie back to let her
know I'll swing by after school, and when I look up, my room
is filled with kids and I need to start teaching.

The bell rings, and before announcements even start, Caleb
in the front row asks, "Did you really go on a date with Ben
Olson this weekend?"

I blow out a breath.

So that's how this Monday is going to go.

And that is how it goes. It starts with Caleb asking me about
Ben, and pretty much every class walks in tittering with the
gossip. I'm asked whether he's my boyfriend. I'm asked
whether we're faking a relationship for the media. I'm asked if
I've been to his house, been in his car, and met his dog. And
these are just the questions my students—and other teachers—
have asked me to my face. Don't even get me started on the
gossip mill or the things I've heard in passing.

By the way, middle school kids are freaking *perverts*.

So it's really no surprise that Janet and Mr. Delnor walk into
my room during the last period of the day. I shut down all
questions and put the focus on my lesson, but still, it's even

42

less of a surprise that they stay until the final student walks out of the room.

"Have a seat," Mr. Delnor says, and he and Janet both stand over me as I sit in a student desk like a child.

"Ms. Dalton, you're becoming quite the distraction to our school community here," Janet begins.

I press my lips together. "I'm so sorry. I didn't think what I do in my personal life would have any bearing on my ability to teach."

"Clearly it does," Janet says snidely. "We can't have our teachers paraded around the gossip sites and maintain an environment of learning."

Blood pounds through my veins angrily, but I maintain a calm exterior as I nod. "That's fine because I won't be returning next year."

She looks neither surprised nor taken aback at my announcement. "Oh, Ms. Dalton. Are you absolutely sure? Your teaching abilities have come so far this year and—"

I hold up a hand because fuck her. I've learned a lot this year—not from her, mind you—and one of the most important lessons is that I'm not cut out for teaching middle school language arts.

Which is why I'm about to light every fucking bridge on fire as I leave this place.

"Save it, Janet. No job is worth what you've put me through this year, and it's really unfortunate for this school that you turned me into the enemy. I have a lot of pride in my workplace, and I would've been more than happy to invite my brothers or my *new boyfriend* to help out with the football team or for charity events. They'd do anything for me, and if I asked them to donate a state of the art gym, they would've done it. If I told them how badly we needed new textbooks, they would've helped out wherever they could. But instead you cast your judgment and decided I wasn't fit to teach at your school. You won." I stand from the chair they forced me into. "I'm leaving when the school year ends, and I'm taking my teaching abilities that *have come so far* along with my very charitable brothers and boyfriend with me somewhere else." I walk back toward my desk and toss my final words over my shoulder without looking at them. "Thanks for the opportunity. You can go now."

I'm sure they're both standing there flabbergasted, but I don't bother to look. I hear the door click shut and I do a gleeful little victory dance.

It was a tough road making this decision, but I'm positive it was the right one.

Especially now that I have a plan. Not only do I get to have a fun competition and raise money for charity with the very sexy Ben Olson, I also get to plan an entire fitness program that could have ripple effects all over the United States.

Things are sure starting to look up...even though I need to jet over to Ellie's and figure out how to put a pin in this Billy Peters business.

"Come on in," Ellie says when she opens the door upon my arrival, and I follow her through the house toward her office. Ben's already sitting on the purple couch in there and Kate's working at her desk.

"Hey boyfriend," I say brightly.

"Hey," he says, nodding at me. "How was school?"

"I told Janet I'm not coming back."

"You did?" Ellie and Kate gasp at the same time.

Ben grins. "That's my girl."

"I also burned all the bridges by letting them know I was taking my charitable brothers and boyfriend with me. Oh, and I told her no job was worth what she put me through this year."

Ben holds up a hand, and I high-five him with a smile then sink down beside him.

"How do we handle this gossip snap video thing?" I ask Ellie.

"How did it even get out?" Ben asks. "Who's the source close to us?"

"My best guess is Shannon," Ellie says. She sighs as she sits at her desk, and she tucks some hair behind her ear. She glances a little nervously at Kate, who nods at her, and then back at Ben and me.

"First, can I just say how good you two look in that picture Billy obtained?" She smiles, and I get the feeling she's trying to butter us up for whatever her plan is. "And you two are good at faking it. Like *really good*. Ben, the way you're looking at Kaylee in this one…" She turns her computer screen around to show us one of the photos. "It really looks like you two are in love. Or at least like you've seen each other naked."

Kate barks out a laugh from her desk near the windows while Ben and I remain silent.

Ellie raises a brow when neither of us responds. "Have you seen each other naked?"

"No!" I exclaim, and Ben just laughs.

"She wishes."

I push his shoulder, which doesn't even make him budge. "Do not."

Ellie laughs. "Okay, so anyway, back to our game plan here. It depends what you want to do, but we have a couple of options. Each comes with a host of pluses and minuses, and I'm here to help talk you through them. Option A, we continue with the plan as is and just ignore gossipers like Billy. Obviously a solid choice, but date one already has people waggling their eyebrows."

45

"Waggling?" Ben repeats. He glances at me. "Is that a word?"

I shrug. "Sure. Like wiggling plus wagging. Waggling."

Ben raises his brows, clearly impressed. "Huh. Learn something new every day."

"Option B," Ellie continues, "we scrap the whole plan and you just took your friend's sister to an event, no big deal."

"A lot of cons there," I say. "We've made a whole plan for the charity thing, which I want to talk to you about next."

"Ben?" Ellie asks, turning toward him.

"Huh?" He's obviously not paying attention.

I elbow him in the ribs. "Do you agree Option B isn't really an option?"

"Yeah, sure. Fine." He shakes his head like he doesn't really care. "What's C?"

"Option C," Ellie says, and clearly this is the one she rehearsed since she glances over at Kate for approval. "We take your relationship to the next level."

My brows push together. "What does that mean?" I ask at the same time Ben says, "Like we have sex in public?"

I elbow Ben in the ribs. "That is so not Option C."

Kate's giggling at her desk. "You two are too much."

"Maybe you're not just *dating*," Ellie says, emphasizing her last word. "Maybe it's more serious than that."

Ben chokes on something as her words start to register.

I clear my throat as I try to grasp onto what she means. "You mean we get fake engaged?" My wheels start to turn.

An engagement would pique the interest of our followers, and piqued interest would only mean good things for our charity.

In the interest of raising more money—and of beating Ben in our little competition—my mind goes to all things bride. The dress. The hair. The honeymoon outfits. The rehearsal dinner. Venues and vendors who would pay top dollar to be showcased on our little corner of the internet.

She raises a brow. "Would that be so bad? Like what does it change, *really*? And if you're so inclined, an actual wedding would *really* shut those critics up."

Ben blanches as I gasp. "You want us to get *married*?" The engagement idea was interesting, but to do it for real?

I don't know about that.

"Not for real," she says. "But nobody would have to know it's not real. It's easy to fake weddings these days. A little photo shoot, a nice white dress, you each wear a ring...and boom! Everyone thinks you're married."

Ben stands. "No. Not a chance in *hell*. I'm not getting married. I'm not *pretending* to be married. I'm not *pretending* to be *planning* to be married." He walks toward the door and turns around for a parting shot. "Get all those thoughts of weddings and engagements the fuck out of your head now because it's not happening." He leaves the room.

"Well that went well," Ellie says. She dusts her hands together like that particular matter is taken care of, but it's not.

My wheels are still turning despite Ben's reaction. "You really think it'll fix things?" I ask. "If we were married, or if people thought we were?"

She shakes her head. "Probably not. It was just an idea."

"Could someone slip to the press that we got married in private without having to do the photo shoot and the white dress and all that?" I ask.

She shrugs and glances at Kate. "I suppose that could work, but you'd be missing out on a lot of potential."

I nod. She's right. Besides, critics would balk if we faked a wedding in secret, and we'd have even more accusations that it was fake if we didn't put it on a stage for the world to see.

"And if the truth comes out, you'd be in an even bigger mess," Kate points out.

Ellie nods. "True. So if you want to take your relationship to the next level, you'd have to either get engaged publicly or actually tie the knot."

"Let me think about it, okay? You know how against a fake wedding I was for you and Luke," I say to Ellie. "I just don't like the idea of lying to everybody."

"I didn't either, but you do what you have to do to protect the people you love." She shrugs. "And I know you and Ben are just friends, if that even, but your brother is his best friend and he's practically family."

"Yeah," I murmur. That's only a part of why I feel like I'm at a crossroads here. The other part is because I actually *am* falling for him, and fake marrying him would only be setting myself up for emotional suicide later.

But what's that old saying? It's better to have loved and lost than to never have loved at all.

Seems like a bunch of malarkey, and certainly it doesn't apply to marriage. There's probably a reason why "it's better to be married and divorced than never to have been married at all" isn't a real saying.

Still, though, it might be worth it just for a few blissful months with Ben Olson. At least doing it this way, I'll have the ability to brace myself for the end.

"I'll talk to him," I say. I just don't have any idea if I'll actually be able to convince him.

CHAPTER 7

Ben

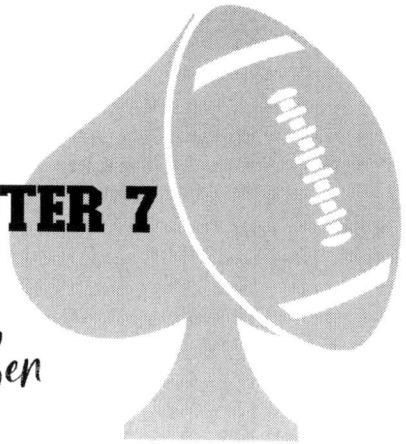

I'm pacing in the kitchen when Kaylee finds me. My heart still thumps loudly in my chest but the rushing buzz in my brain has calmed.

I want nothing to do with marriage or engagements or commitment. I don't even like attending weddings when they're for *other people*.

And now Ellie thinks Kaylee and I need to get married to continue this charade? I wasn't even on board for the girlfriend idea. The only reason I agreed was to get Calvin off my back. It has nothing to do with Kaylee's magical pussy.

And the only reason I'd even consider continuing with it after this first Billy Peters hiccup is because of the charity idea and what kind of impact we could have on kids and future athletics. Together, Kaylee and I could raise a ton of cash, and I'm also helping out the little sister of a buddy by getting her out of a career she can't stand and laying out a new one for her. But she needs my help for that.

I even like the competition idea she came up with. It doesn't matter who wins it in the end since the goal is to raise money for a cause, but I'm highly competitive by nature. I want to win—probably as much, if not more, than she does.

And the thing that scared me maybe most of all when Ellie mentioned an engagement or marriage to Kaylee Dalton was the first thought that flashed through my mind before the fear stepped in.

I don't want to think it again.

I can't.

It's not me, and it's not where I ever saw my life headed—real or pretend.

And yet…

I draw in a deep breath as I try to calm my racing heart.

I didn't hate the idea as much as I felt like I needed to act like I did. As much as I still feel the need to act like I do.

The thought of Kaylee in a white dress walking down the aisle toward me, of a honeymoon spent mostly naked, of a future where she's taking the lead over a fitness class for kids at *my* gym, of her wrapped like a vine around my body every night as we fall asleep together as husbands and wives do…all that should scare me. Instead it does something else to me.

And *that* is what's so goddamn terrifying about all this.

"You okay?" Kaylee asks cautiously.

I blow out a breath as I pause my pacing to face the windows. I stare out at Luke and Ellie's backyard. It's a family yard filled with kid toys that probably weren't there before little Nolan came along but are certainly center stage now.

Marriage, kids…it's all a universe I've never wanted any part of. I think back to when I was a kid and my parents were fighting all the time. I was ten, old enough to understand what was going on, and listening to them was enough to turn me off to ever wanting that for myself.

And then Tatum came along.

She convinced me over time that I *did* want that, though the gift of hindsight tells a different story. The truth is that *she* wanted it, and she convinced me I did, too.

But I never really did…not until a blue-eyed girl turned into a woman I can't stop thinking about. And it's not just her ass I can't stop thinking about, though that does take up more than its fair share of real estate in my brain.

She's beautiful, yes. Hot as fuck too.

But she's smart. She's funny. She's kind. She puts her family first. She's caring and, like me, wants to make a difference in her short time in this world, but she can be a shark when she wants to be, or a firecracker, or a fucking tiger.

And for as much as I tried to convince myself feelings wouldn't get involved…they're involved.

There are a whole lot of implications that go along with that admission, though, which is why I need to keep it close to the vest. I need to work my way through it so we can focus on the deal we made.

"Yeah," I grunt. "I'm fine." I turn to face her, and she doesn't have quite the same look of terror in her eyes that I'm feeling, but she doesn't exactly look calm, either. "What are your thoughts on their idea?"

She shrugs. "Honestly my mind went to the charity first. Imagine the sponsorship opportunities for both of us if we're planning a wedding." She air quotes *planning a wedding* as if that lessens the weight of the words. It doesn't.

"There are other ways to make money," I say flatly.

She walks across the room until she's standing beside me, and she looks out over the yard. I turn to look at the view, too. "Yeah, there are. And there's an awful lot about all this that goes against everything I believe in. But I don't want to give up on this plan yet. Do you?"

I focus on a bush clear across the yard. I don't know what it's called, nor do I care. It's some round bush with pink flowers all over it, and that's the type of shit husbands and fathers know. If I asked Luke, I'm sure he'd come in with the title and its complete life cycle along with the exact amount of daily water it requires to flourish.

That's not shit I want to know. Ever.

And while I've admitted to myself that the place where I'm currently located in life isn't where I belong for very much longer, the dad who knows the name of every plant in his backyard isn't where I'm taking my life next.

But as I glance down at Kaylee, I can't help but wonder whether she has the power to flip everything I ever believed on its head. Maybe she knows the names of the plants and I won't have to learn them. Maybe that's what a true partnership really is—allowing each of us to have our own strengths so that together we can hold onto each other and face this world.

Maybe she's the piece that's been missing all this time as I've settled into a life on my own and tried to become everything to everybody while I've lost sight of what I might actually need to make myself whole.

"What's that bush called?" I ask, pointing to the one I've been studying by way of experimentation. If she doesn't know the answer, then maybe all these random thoughts I'm having can just be shoved back into the dark recesses where they came from.

But if she does…then maybe she's that piece I didn't know I was missing.

"Dwarf oleander." Her words come without missing a single beat.

Oh shit.

I am so fucked.

CHAPTER 8

Kaylee

He turns away from the window. His shoulders are hitched up and I'm hearing a lot of heavy sighs coming from him, a clear indication that he's torn over what to do.

"Hey," I say softly. I reach over and touch his forearm. "We don't need to make any decisions right now. So one gossip assclown accused us of faking it. Who cares? We go out again and show that we're not faking, and we get cozy in public so people can snap our picture and we can prove it's real. What do we have to lose?"

He nods, a bit of calmness allowing his shoulders to sag with comfort at my words.

"Whatever we decide, we'll talk it through and make the best choice for *us*. Okay?" I squeeze his arm.

He heaves out another breath and glances at me with a bit of wonder in his eyes. "Okay." He presses his lips together then leans down and plants a soft kiss on my cheek. "Thank you."

"Of course." My eyes are on him as he backs away, and I wish we were at his place so I could leap into his arms and hold him and calm his fears.

But we're not. We're at Luke and Ellie's, a place where the people inside have no idea what's really happening between us.

Hell, I'm not even sure if *I* understand what's happening between us. "We're in this together, and we're going to raise a bunch of money to put our fitness for kids plan into action regardless of whether that includes a wedding."

He nods. "And I'm going to kick your ass in our little competition."

"Pfft," I scoff as we both work to lighten the mood in here a little. "Good luck, pal."

He laughs, and all that marriage talk is pushed to the backburner...for now at least. Because even though that's where we've put it, it's still on my mind.

And I'm not ready to give up on it just yet.

We head back to Ellie's office.

"I'm taking off," Ben announces.

Ellie nods. "We'll come up with something."

Ben presses his lips together and nods a goodbye before he turns and walks out, and I plop down on the purple couch. "I gave your job offer some thought, and I think I want to take you up on it."

"You do?" Ellie asks, clearly surprised.

I nod. "I figure I can swing by after school for an hour or so each day to start to learn the ropes, and once school's out, I can move into whatever role you want me to take. I'm ready to learn the basics of public relations."

Ellie's brows dip. "Why the sudden change of heart?"

I lift a shoulder. "I posed an Instagram challenge to Ben, a sort of competition to raise money for charity, and the more I know about the sort of tactics you employ, the better my shot at winning."

Ellie's eyes light with excitement. "Tell me more about this competition."

I launch into the basics, obviously leaving out the stakes of the loser planning a mystery date for the winner. She nods as I talk about a different sort of engagement than she just did—this one is interacting on social media rather than committing to marriage.

"I think it's an incredible idea," Ellie says. "And I promise to be an impartial party to your competition. I'll give you equal tools to work with and you can decide which ones to use."

I issue a glare. "I mean you *could* help tip the scales in my favor since I'm your favorite sister-in-law."

Kate clears her throat loudly from her spot across the room, and I roll my eyes good-naturedly.

"Top two?" I ask, and Kate laughs.

"You're both in my top two," Ellie says, and she blows us each kisses. "Now grab a chair and start shadowing Kate. She's working on creating some captions from sound bites right now, something you'll be doing once she graduates and you slide into her role. And after that, I need to chat with you about a game plan to build your following so we can raise a boatload of cash for your charity."

Kate waves me over, and suddenly I'm really excited about my new job prospect.

* * *

"So you two are a couple now?" my mom asks the second I walk through her front door. Ben is already there with Jack, and I arrived with Luke, Ellie, and Kate. We wait until the door is closed behind us *just in case* anybody's hanging around outside to address that particular topic.

"I agreed to pose as Ben's girlfriend," I explain. "His boss wanted him to clean up his image a little, and everyone agreed I had nothing else going on."

"Oh, Kay," my mom says, her tone sympathetic as she looks at me sadly.

"It's fine," I say, shrugging her off. "We're just having fun with it and I'm going to get a lot of amazing meals out of it."

"And drinks," Ben chimes in. "Just because I'm tied down now doesn't mean I won't still party."

I smack him in the arm. "You're sort of totally missing the point of what we're doing."

My mom laughs. "Just take care of her, Ben. She's my little girl."

My cheeks burn. I'm so sick and tired of being cast as the *little girl*. And it's beyond embarrassing to be labeled that in front of Ben. "I'm not little anymore," I grit out between a clenched jaw, but it falls on deaf ears as everyone starts moving in toward the kitchen.

"You most certainly are not," Ben murmurs, and he heads up the back of the pack just behind me. He grabs my ass, and I let out a little yelp and a giggle as I jump and turn around. "So peachy," he whispers.

I laugh, and I cross my fingers we'll have some time to fool around under the table.

Unfortunately, though, we do not.

Instead, the attention is on the two of us as we field questions about how we're going to handle this fake relationship.

And somehow, the more my family fires questions at us and the more we seem to easily agree on the answers, the more this is starting to feel less *fake* and more real.

CHAPTER 9

Kaylee

I'm getting ready for bed a little earlier than usual since I have an early morning parent meeting tomorrow when a text from Ben comes through.

Trouble: *Can we talk?*

Me: *Want to come over?*

Trouble: *Probably better if you come here. You know, better potential for naked time.*

Me: *I have a seven o'clock parent meeting tomorrow.*

Trouble: *So you'll go with a smile on your face. Bring an overnight bag.*

I sigh. It's a bad idea, but at least we can blame our fake relationship if anyone in my family catches me hanging at Ben's place off-hours.

Me: *Give me a few minutes.*

Trouble: *[eggplant emoji] [two finger peace sign emoji] [water droplets emoji] [smiley face emoji]*

I giggle at his text and catch myself staring at it a few extra beats.

God, I'm really falling for him.

It's stupid.

I shouldn't be.

But I am.

I sigh then grab a duffel bag with a change of clothes for the morning plus all the essentials, and then I head downstairs.

"Where are you going?" Jack asks me. He's flipping through some paperwork at the kitchen table.

"Ben's," I answer honestly. "We agreed if someone catches me sneaking in late or leaving early or sees my car parked in his driveway overnight, all the better for our cause." None of that's a lie.

"Have fun," he says absently, and I hate that I feel like I'm lying to my brother through omission.

"You too. Enjoy your empty house with your wife and your sleeping baby." I toss him an exaggerated wink, and his laughter follows me out the door to my car.

When I get to Ben's place, I spot a car I've never seen before parked across the street. I haven't been here that many times, but enough to know I don't recognize whoever it is. There's definitely a figure sitting in the front seat, and while I'm certain I'm safe…it still feels a little creepy.

I decide to text Ben.

Me: *I'm here and someone's sitting in their car across the street.*

His front door opens seconds later, and he stands there without a shirt on and just those glorious gray shorts as he waves me in. I grab my overnight bag and exit my car.

"Let's give them a show," he says softly as I approach, and my eyes flick down to his chest first, then to his abs, and a little lower still before I raise a brow and grin. He meets me on his front porch and grabs me into his arms. His mouth crashes down to mine, and this is one of those moments when I really don't have to put on a show even though I hope whoever's across the street is getting good pictures they can use to help our cause.

He pulls me into his house, our lips still connected, and he slams the door behind me. I'm expecting him to pull back once

58

the door latches shut, but he doesn't. Instead, he shoves his hips against mine as he backs me up into the door. He deepens our kiss, turning the little spark into an urgent, raging inferno.

I pull back first. "Didn't you invite me over to talk?" I ask, my voice breathless.

He doesn't chuckle like I expect him to. Instead, he nips my lips with his then says, "It can wait."

I agree.

My hand immediately goes to his shorts, where I find exactly what I'm looking for. He drives his hips against my hand, and I feel how hard and ready he is for me. I massage him over those shorts as he moans into our kiss.

And then he shoves a hand down my jeans and gets to work.

I groan into him as he pushes one of those long fingers into me, and I start rubbing his length on the outside of his shorts. His grunts spur me on until I reach into his shorts and grasp him in my fist. I move my fist up and down his shaft then reach a little lower to cup his balls, and he growls at me, the sound both feral and sexy.

He pulls his finger out of me to rub my clit, then he removes his hand completely from my jeans.

"Get naked. Now." He reaches into the pocket of his shorts once I get my hand out of them so I can take off my jeans, and then pulls off his shorts and Bart Simpson boxers and rolls on a condom.

His mouth crashes down to mine as he lifts me up so our hips are aligned. I wrap my legs around his waist and my arms around his neck as he reaches under me to grip himself. A moment later, he's moving inside me.

I lean my head back until it thumps against the front door, and I see stars as he fucks me against his door in his foyer.

It's not the first time we've had foyer door sex, though it *is* the first time here at his house we've done this. His fingers are splayed under my thighs, and he inches his hands back until he's gripping my ass in both hands. He slides one of his hands over a little, his fingertips brushing against my back door, and I clench up front at the surprise sensation.

He lets out a loud roar as my body tightens over his, and as he continues to shove up into me, he pulls back.

"Open your eyes," he says.

I do, and his are full of mischief.

"I want to watch your face while I do this," he murmurs between grunts.

"Do what?" I ask, my voice breathless and he pushes a finger into my asshole.

I clench again as he continues to drive into me, and I squeal out some incomprehensible sound as a new sensation leaps through me.

I thought it would be gross…but it's not. It's different and it's strange and it's really freaking *hot*.

I keep my eyes open as he gently moves his finger in and out back there and continues to thrust his giant cock into me. I lose all sense as the buildup of pleasure plows into me, and I scream out incoherently as I climax harder than I've ever climaxed in my life.

My body is out of control as it jerks and twists and contracts over him, and he removes his finger as I continue to ride the wave. My eyes must've closed at some point, and as the peak starts to wane, they fly open so I can watch his face, too. His is twisted in pleasure, and his neck is corded as it's tipped back. "Fuck!" he growls as he pumps into me a little faster, and then he roars before he starts to slow his drives.

His eyes open, and there's a sense of calm there as they meet mine. I feel like jelly as he slips out of me and lowers me down to the ground, and he kisses me one more time as he wraps his arms around me and drops a soft kiss to my shoulder.

"Well that was unexpected," I say, my words reminiscent of the first time we did that same thing up against Jack's front door as I pick up my bra. I toss it near my duffel bag and slip my shirt over my head as he pulls his shorts back on.

This time he does chuckle. "What can I say? Expect the unexpected with me."

"Does it seem like it gets better each time?" I ask as I grab my panties and pull them on.

His eyes dart to mine, and I spot a little fear there. I'm not sure why, though.

He clears his throat. "Yeah, it does. And I guess that's why I called you over."

My brows dip as I finish getting dressed. "To test the theory that it gets better each time?"

He shakes his head. "I, uh…I don't usually do this."

"Fake a relationship for the public while you're secretly banging your best friend's little sister? Yeah, I'd say this is a first for me, too."

He twists his lips and cocks his head, and I follow him into the family room. He collapses onto the couch then pats the cushion next to him, and I sit. I curl my legs under me and face him.

He clears his throat as he threads his fingers together, and then he works his fingers together as he squeezes knuckle against knuckle, his eyes on his hands as he fidgets. He straightens both hands and rubs them together before he folds them and does the knuckle thing again. Clearly he's nervous about whatever it is he wants to say.

"What's up, Ben?" I ask lightly.

He presses his lips together then stretches his legs out to prop his feet up on the coffee table. He clasps his hands behind his head and leans back to stare up at the ceiling.

"This is all just a lot," he finally says. "It feels like it's getting serious when that's not what we agreed to."

"It's not getting more serious," I say cautiously. He's right, though. I mean, hell, we were talking about *marriage* earlier today.

"Babe, you just said it gets better every time," he argues as he turns toward me, and I don't miss his term of endearment, "and I couldn't disagree with that statement. But that's the thing. I don't sleep with one woman enough times to know if it's supposed to get better or if this is an anomaly. I figured it was fine to keep boning since we're doing this fake thing anyway, but there's no way to do this and guarantee feelings won't get involved."

Oh, we're long past that point, but right now hardly feels like the time to admit it. "Of course we can't guarantee that. When it comes to feelings and emotions, there are *never* guarantees. But whatever happens, Ben, I can handle it."

He nods and returns his gaze to the ceiling. "Me too."

But something in his voice—or maybe it's the way he's avoiding eye contact with me—tells me he's not giving me the whole truth. I guess I have the next five months to figure out what that truth is.

CHAPTER 10

Ben

Her words that she can handle it should make me feel better.

They don't.

Instead, I feel a little disappointed.

What the fuck is that?

I've been very clear about what I want. I want to remain detached. I want to keep this casual. I just want to have some fun.

But feelings are getting in the way already, and my instinct is to run. We should scrap this whole *relationship for the media* plan and run far as fuck away from each other. This is Jack's little sister. I saw how he almost had a hernia when Cory Marshall mentioned something as simple as asking Kaylee out for a drink. I can't imagine how protective he'd get over an animal like me wanting to get into something serious with her.

The problem is that he still sees her as a little girl, the sweet, innocent sister. And ever since their father passed away, he's taken on the role of her father figure. I get him wanting to be protective over her even though I don't personally have any siblings to feel protective over or otherwise.

But the way he still sees her—it's not her. She's none of those things. Sweet—maybe sometimes. Little and innocent? Not so much.

As proven by the way she fucks, among other things.

I get it, though. He doesn't want some asshole like me to break her heart. He knows how she feels about football players, and I don't blame her for wanting something different out of life.

But I can't play football forever, and I'm not planning to go the coaching route upon retirement, though broadcasting might be fun…but more than likely she's safe with me when it comes to not wanting the game to be her life for the rest of time. I'd estimate a few more years max.

In other ways, though…she's definitely not safe when it comes to me.

I'm not used to any of this, so when she starts yawning, things take a bit of an awkward turn. "Do you, uh, want to go to bed?" I ask.

"I need to. I have an early meeting and you just worked me over. I'll be exhausted tomorrow, but that was definitely worth it."

I nod. "You can sleep in my room if you want."

"If I want?" she echoes. She looks confused for a beat. "That's the plan, isn't it?"

"Well, yeah, but if you want to stay in the guest room…"

"Do you *want* me to stay in the guest room?" she counters.

I feel like I stepped on her toes and I was just trying to be nice. I try to backtrack. "No! I just, I mean——" Oh hell. I have no idea what the fuck I mean. "I just want you to be comfortable here."

She leans in toward me and presses a kiss to my cheek. "I'm just teasing you. This is just casual, right? I'll sleep on the freaking couch if it helps you feel a little less awkward."

I shoot her a sheepish smile. "Am I that obvious?"

She nods. "Beyond obvious. I know this is unconventional, but like I've already said, we'll manage this however works best for us."

"Do you really think a wedding would help us raise money?" I ask. I realize my question comes out of the blue, but I feel like it's a question I need the answer to.

She lifts a shoulder. "I think it would only strengthen our cause. I dislike the idea of lying about it, but I really do see a ton of potential with it."

I press my lips together. "What if you, I don't know…just like drop hints about a possible wedding?"

"What do you mean?" She tilts her head as she asks, and every time she does that, a strange wave passes across my chest.

She's not just gorgeous and hot and fuckable. She's *cute*, too. And I've never found anything about a woman *cute* before.

Hot, yes.

Fuckable, definitely.

But cute? Never.

"I don't know. Never mind." I shake the idea right out of my head.

"Don't give me that, Olson." She tugs on my arm.

I blow out a breath. "What if you posted a photo from one of those stores that sells wedding dresses? Or were caught buying magazines with brides on them? Just shit like that. Dropping hints to give them something to talk about."

She raises her brows. "Hey, now that's not a bad idea. Let me chat about it with Ellie tomorrow and we'll put together a game plan." She narrows her eyes at me. "But you do realize this will give me an advantage, don't you?"

My brows dip. "What will?"

"Posting about wedding stuff. Dropping hints. People will flock to me so they can get an inside look at *you*."

I hadn't thought about that.

It's just another example of how we fit so well together. She makes up for what I lack, and maybe vice versa, though I can't think of a damn thing she lacks.

It's in that moment when a new thought comes to mind. I'm starting to move into this new territory where I feel like I don't want to have any regrets versus being too scared to take a risk with her.

I don't want to leave any *what if*s out there. What if we *are* meant to be more than just casual? What if I've closed myself off for something more this whole time when all it took was the right woman to come along and open that possibility up?

I'm starting to feel like I *have* to do this with her. I *have* to give it a real shot. No woman has ever made me *want* to before, but when I think about what it would look like not to talk to her every day…

My stomach twists violently at just the mere thought.

Yeah, this definitely ain't just casual anymore. But just because I'm starting to feel unfamiliar things doesn't mean we need to label anything just yet.

And so as she leans over and presses a kiss to my mouth then bids me goodnight as she heads up the stairs to my bed, I don't say a thing. I do, however, keep my eyes on her sweet, peachy ass until she turns the corner.

We're fine to keep chugging along as we have been. Feelings can grow, but they can die just as easily, as proven by my history. Nothing needs to change right now—in fact, if anything, it would be stupid to admit my feelings are in transition since we're tied into this deal for the next five months. If she doesn't feel the same, it'll only hurt what we're doing. Or if she *does* feel the same and we give it a real try and it doesn't work out, that'll fuck our deal, too.

So I'll keep my mouth shut for now. And if those feelings continue to grow…well, I guess we can figure out what to do about them when our deal is up.

CHAPTER 11

Kaylee

I'm comfortable when my alarm on my phone starts ringing.

Too comfortable. *Way* too comfortable. Like I could lie here all day and be perfectly content in this cocoon.

It feels like a dream here, and for a second, I think it is until I remember I slept in Ben Olson's bed last night.

If only this were just a dream and not real life, then I really would lie here all day…but duty calls.

I'm warm and cozy, and I let the sound of the beeping fill the air a little too long because eventually the person whose arms I'm wrapped in shifts and a deep voice rasps hoarsely at me. "Are you gonna turn that damn thing off?"

I giggle, and I admit it's a little concerning how good it feels waking up in Ben's arms. "I told you it was going to be an early morning."

"You can take the guest room next time if you're a snoozer," he mutters.

"A snoozer?" I ask, regrettably sitting up and moving out of his arms. I grab my phone and turn off the alarm, but the screen lights the room for a beat.

He shifts and tosses an arm over his eyes. "One who presses the snooze button."

"Isn't everybody a snoozer?" I don't know that I've ever shared a bed or a room with someone who wasn't. Each of my college roommates was, and Dane was, too. Apart from those examples, I haven't really experienced many mornings with alarm clocks belonging to other people.

"Some of us hop right out of bed at the first sound of the alarm to get a start on our day," he argues. "You know, at a reasonable hour."

"Well not everybody loves their job the way you do," I point out. "Besides, I'd hardly call five-thirty unreasonable." I lean over and press a kiss to his scruffy cheek, though admittedly it *is* about a half hour earlier than I usually get up…and I did go to bed about an hour later than normal.

He turns his head and catches my lips. "Let's agree to disagree on that one."

I giggle as I get out of bed and locate my duffel bag. "Since you're up, I wouldn't say no to a pot of coffee." It's not my preferred beverage of choice. I typically prefer Diet Dr Pepper for my energy boost, but one time I heard my brother say that he doesn't trust anybody who doesn't start the day with a cup of coffee, and if Ben feels the same way…well, I don't want to make a bad impression for our first *planned* sleepover.

He laughs as I disappear into the bathroom, and I'm frankly shocked to smell coffee as I walk down the stairs toward the kitchen a half hour later once I'm dressed and ready for the day.

And it isn't just coffee I smell. "What's that delicious smell?" I ask as I walk into the room.

"My cock," he deadpans.

I roll my eyes.

"Homemade raspberry chocolate croissants," he clarifies.

"Homemade? As in you took them out of the freezer and made them?"

He laughs and shakes his head. "It's my Gramma Jean's recipe. She taught me how to cook."

My brows arch. "You can *cook?*"

He shrugs. "I have many talents. So far you've only really been introduced to the sexual ones."

I laugh. "I don't think that's true. I've seen you play football, too, and smash beer cans on your forehead. And you can wear the hell out of a pair of gray shorts."

He nods. "All true. And I can also cook." He hands me a plate with one of his croissants and a couple slices of bacon. "Figured you'd want something with protein to give you strength for your early morning meeting plus something sweet to start the day off with a smile, and since I didn't know if we'd have time for sex, I made the next best thing."

I eye the croissant. "You're comparing a breakfast pastry to your prowess in bed?"

"You haven't tasted it yet." He nods as if to give me the green light, and I pick up the warm croissant and take a bite.

And I nearly orgasm on the spot. "Oh my God, Ben," I say as the flavors melt together in a delightful little fusion in my mouth. "This is fantastic."

He brushes off his shoulders. "Told you. And you're totally making your O face right now, which only proves my point that these are the next best thing to sex."

"I can't argue with you there," I admit. "But really? *This* is my O face?" I twist my face up again as I take another bite, and he shifts.

"Yep. Definitely the same face. How much time did you say you have until you need to leave?"

I check the clock. "About ten minutes."

"I only need two."

I take another bite of the delicious pastry then start undoing my pants. "Then start my day with an even bigger smile on my face, Olson."

He laughs, and then he does.

The smile lasts through the parent meeting, which goes as smoothly as one can hope these things will go, through my morning classes when kids ask me left and right if I'm really dating Ben Olson, through yet another surprise observation from Janet even though I'm not coming back next year and frankly whatever I do for the next week and a half before school ends is pretty much meaningless, and all the way through my afternoon classes, too.

In fact, the smile doesn't fade at all until my classroom door opens at half past three, just as I'm shuffling the last of my papers for the day and getting ready to grab my purse out of my bottom drawer to head home.

I assume it'll be one of the teachers in my department I've gotten semi-friendly with, or maybe Jason from Social Studies back to beg for tickets to a game.

And when I spot who's on the other side of the door, my jaw drops open.

It's not Jason. It's not Kristen and it's not Ashley. It's not Janet or Mr. Delnor. It's not a teacher at all.

"Dane," I mutter, all the blood draining from my face. "What are you doing here?"

The voice I haven't heard in nearly a year is as steady as it ever was. "We need to talk."

CHAPTER 12

Kaylee

"What exactly do we need to talk about?" I can't ignore the feelings that plow into me as my ex stands in the doorway of my classroom.

I never even dreamed he'd show up in Vegas, let alone track me down at my place of work.

"I just realized some things over the last couple months and felt like it was a conversation we should have in person."

I blow out a breath. We didn't end on bad terms, but it still hurt when we ended things. I had imagined a future with him for a long time, and now he's standing here in front of me. I wish I could say I don't feel anything, but that's just not true.

But I'm not exactly sure *what* I'm feeling.

I have in front of me the man who I thought was going to give me the future I wanted. Meanwhile I woke up in the bed of a man who has made zero indication that he's willing to have the sort of future I want. So I'm basically wasting my time with him while I figure out my life.

But I'm starting to figure it out at this point.

I quit my job. I know I don't want to teach anymore, and that's okay.

It's okay to rely on the money my dad left for me to start building the future I want.

The realizations of both those things were major game changers for me.

And I'm liking this Instagram idea more and more. I don't have to give anything up when it comes to my privacy just because I have a wider following. I choose what they see of me.

With people like Ellie and Kate on my side to offer guidance and suggestions in particular when it comes to life in the public eye and building a platform to monetize, I can have any sort of future I want. Ben was right when he suggested I lean into the advantages I have where my brothers are concerned rather than running so hard away from the types of doors that could be opened for me simply because of the family I was born into. Even though I wanted to shy away from football, I still have a passion for athletics. This idea with Ben's gym and the charity gives me a new purpose. Raising money for charity feels good and right.

And now, instead of feeling like I'm at a dead end, stuck in a career I don't even like, I feel excited. I feel a renewed energy. I feel like the sky is the limit.

I've gotten used to and excited for this idea of the future…but now my past is walking back in.

"Okay," I finally say. "Go ahead and say what you need to say."

He glances around my classroom. "Here?"

I lift a shoulder. "You came all this way."

He tilts his head as he studies me, and I realize he's never seen this side of me. But he didn't have to, and maybe I've never seen this side of me, either. I've never been the strong, outspoken one because I let everyone else dictate my life for me.

But I've grown up a lot over the last year, and I'm figuring out who I am as I find my place in the world. And I've done all that without Dane by my side.

"You want to go grab some coffee?" Dane asks.

I move to grab my purse to take him up on that when I realize I can't just go out for coffee with him. People are watching now, and I have an image to portray.

And it's not just that.

I don't even really drink coffee that often. He knows this. If I need a quick burst of energy, I typically reach for Diet Dr Pepper. I had a cup of coffee this morning at Ben's, and that was my limit one on the day.

"Let's just talk here," I say. I pick up my stack of papers and arrange them into a neater pile as he nods.

He closes my classroom door and walks fully into the room. He walks toward my desk, stopping to perch on top of the student desk closest to mine.

He lets out a soft chuckle. "You always said your desk would be in the back of the room."

I press my lips together. "Then they never know where I'm looking."

"Always one step ahead," he murmurs, my mantra when I was studying to become a teacher.

"That hasn't changed." I clear my throat. "I've got a lot going on. I'm meeting my sister-in-law after school and I need to get going. So tell me what you're doing here."

"Oh come on, Kay," he teases playfully, but this conversation doesn't *feel* playful and his teasing feels misplaced. "Your former boyfriend doesn't get a warmer reception than that?"

"You walk in here unannounced after I haven't seen you in almost a year and you expect me to just drop everything for you?"

He glances away from me and out my windows. "You're right. That was out of line. Is there a better time we can talk?"

I shake my head. "You didn't come all this way to make an appointment."

"Are you angry?" he asks.

"No." I shake my head. "I'm busy."

"Are you seeing somebody?"

That's quite a loaded question. For all intents and purposes, yes, I am. But this is Dane…someone who once knew me better than anybody else. He's someone I would trust with my truth, and yet I find myself unwilling to give it to him.

I focus my eyes straight on him so he doesn't think I'm lying. "Yes, I am."

"So I'm too late," he says flatly.

"Too late for what?"

"This isn't how I pictured this conversation going. I don't know how serious you are with whoever it is you're seeing, but I want you back."

My jaw slackens as I stare at him. "You what?"

He lifts a shoulder. "You heard me. I've done a lot of thinking over the last year as I've gotten a start on my career. When we graduated, I'll admit I got scared. It was a lot of changes all at once and it seemed easier to put my career first. But the harder I work and the more hours I log, the more I wonder why I'm doing this. What's it all for? And the answer to that question is you. It's always been you."

He pauses and waits for my response, but I don't even know what to say.

"I didn't realize it until I went to a buddy from work's house. He's married and has a couple little kids. I wondered why we couldn't just meet at a bar for happy hour like normal coworkers, and I watched as he walked into his house. His kids ran up to him the second he walked through the door. They yelled 'Daddy!' as they leapt into his arms. And it took seeing that to realize it's everything I want." He turns toward me. "With you."

"Why with me?" I ask.

"Because there's nobody like you. There's nobody who cares like you. Who loves like you. Who smiles like you. Who puts others first and makes sacrifices. Who would be the kind of mother to our children they deserve. When I think about those kids running into my arms when I get home from work, the woman standing there smiling as she watches the scene unfold is you."

I blow out a breath. "You know this is coming about eleven months too late, right?"

His face falls a little, and for just a beat I feel bad that the words came out of my mouth.

Because for as much as he knew me better than anyone else, I knew *him*, too. That's what happens when you spend nearly every waking moment with another person. We were in college, in this dreamland just before reality plowed into us. Everything was perfect until it wasn't.

"The guy I'm seeing…it's really serious," I say. Suddenly protecting my lie with Ben feels like the most important thing, even though Dane is standing in front of me now offering me everything I wanted.

"Ben Olson?" he asks softly.

I nod.

"So it wasn't just a media ploy," he says flatly.

I huff out a mirthless chuckle. "No. Not a media ploy," I say. But it's also not an actual serious relationship. It isn't exactly what I'm portraying it to be, not that it matters. The truth is that my feelings are serious.

"How long have you been seeing him?" he asks.

We haven't come up with that particular detail just yet, so I make it up on the spot. "My family has a weekly dinner now that we all live so close to each other. Jack invited him to the first one back in October and he's been coming every week since. We started talking and getting to know one another, and we made it official a couple months ago."

"A couple months, huh?" he asks, and the side of his mouth tips up in a sly smile—the same smile that always brought me to my knees. And as my heart picks up speed, I realize that smile still has the potential to do that. "Then it's not like you're married, and it's not like I'm going to just back down without a fight."

I close my eyes and glance down at my desk. I should've known the second he walked through the door that this wasn't going to be easy. He never made it easy to say no to him. He's stubborn, and it's because of that stubborn streak that we started dating in the first place. He asked me out relentlessly for months after we built a friendship, but I didn't want to ruin what we had.

Eventually I agreed to a date, and he kissed me at the end, and the rest was history. But if he hadn't asked me out so relentlessly, I never would've given him nearly a year of my heart and we wouldn't be sitting here right now.

And a little part of me can't help but wonder if he presses as relentlessly as he did the first time whether he'll come out the victor at the end of this.

So the real question is, which man belongs in my future: Dane or Ben?

CHAPTER 13

Kaylee

"This is all just a lot," I finally say. Part of me just wants him to go while the other part of me—the part of me that fell in love and thought this man was going to be in my life forever—wants him to stay.

And I'm not sure which part to listen to.

What Ben and I are doing is fun, but he was loud and clear last night. He wants to keep things casual. He went so far as to tell me I could sleep in the guest room if I wanted to. He's full of constant reminders that he doesn't want anything more than sex with me, and seeing Dane as he stands in front of me is a reminder that as much fun as I have with Ben, at some point I deserve more than just casual sex…no matter how fun or how good—*great*—it is.

I thought I could do this, that I could manage the casual thing with him…but now that I have an offer for more on the table, I'm confused.

I guess I just wish it was *Ben* who changed his mind and wanted those things even though the decade separating us and his place in my brother's life complicates things between us.

I stare out the window as memories of my history with Dane plow into me. Our first date was our junior year. We met through a mutual friend at a party, and we hung out and cemented a friendship before he asked me out the first time…and the second, third, and fourth times. I issued rejection after rejection, citing our friendship as the reason, but the truth was that I was scared he was just another guy out to use me for my brothers.

He wasn't.

He liked football, but he was really a baseball guy…which made him perfect for me.

I finally agreed to that first date, and we ended up exclusive for a few months. I ended it just before I went home to Michigan for the summer. The night we both finished final exams, we drank a lot of vodka and laughed as we dreamed about the future. But during our drunken escapades, he admitted he didn't want kids.

I couldn't see myself wasting time on a man who didn't want the same sort of future I wanted, and so summer felt like the right time to break it off.

But then a few months later, my dad died.

I leaned on Dane. Even though I knew we wanted different futures, I found myself back together with him. He was comfort at the time I needed it most. But even though we spent the majority of our senior year together, when graduation was upon us, I knew in my heart I couldn't head off into the real world still attached to someone who didn't share the values that were so important to me. I didn't want to do the long-distance thing, and neither did he, and so the day I accepted the job in Vegas——the place I knew I should be since my entire family was there——I ended things with Dane.

"I'll give you some time to think."

"Where are you staying?" I ask.

"Silverton."

I nod. It makes sense he'd stay off-Strip but close. He's frugal in his spending and isn't the likeliest candidate to throw down at a blackjack table, but he's still interested enough to be close to the action.

"I didn't pick it," he clarifies. When my brows knit together in confusion, he adds, "I'm here for a work thing."

Ahh. Well that makes so much more sense then.

Dane was never the guy who'd just show up out of the blue to win me back. He happened to be in town, and he happened to look me up and now he's sitting in my classroom. It's not like he flew clear across the country to see me, and the thought that he didn't…well, it kind of changes things.

"So…you didn't come here to see me?" I ask.

"Of course I did. The second I saw the conference come up at work, I volunteered for it. I *begged* for it. I think in my heart I needed a reason to come out here, like it'd help me save face, but on the flight over, I realized I didn't care about saving face. I only care about you. And even though I have a hotel room, I was hoping we'd reconnect and…" he trails off.

"And I'd invite you to stay with me?"

He shrugs, which just tells me I hit the nail on the head.

"Dane, I hardly know you anymore, and I'm practically living at my boyfriend's place."

He flattens his lips into a thin line. "I understand. I was just hoping we could go to dinner."

"I need to talk it over with Ben," I admit. I finger the edge of my pile of papers.

He raises a brow but doesn't respond, and it's then I realize I probably sound like some insecure girl who needs to check with my boyfriend if it's okay to go out with another guy, but the truth is that given our media situation, I can't just go out to dinner with my ex…and certainly not without checking in with Ben and probably Ellie first.

"It's pretty serious already, huh?" he muses, his eyes down on his hands where they're folded in his lap.

I nod. "We've known each other for a long time." I pick up the pile of papers again.

"I remember," he says. "I just got the impression you weren't into him."

"I wasn't," I admit. I straighten the papers out by tapping the bottom of the pile against the desk. I set them down and look up at my ex. "But feelings change." My tone is pointed, and he nods then stands.

"Some don't."

I clear my throat but don't know what to say to that. He's made his intentions clear.

"Well, you've got my number. At least I assume you still do. I'll be in town until Sunday." His words contradict the previous ones when he said he won't give up without a fight, but I don't really trust that he's going to just sit back and wait for me to call. He's got a plan. I know this because I know *him*. He's nothing if not a planner, and he didn't come to my classroom today with the intent to walk away the loser.

In short, the way Dane sees it, at least, I'm not wearing a wedding ring. That means he still has a chance.

And I need some time to think through whether he's right.

CHAPTER 14

Ben

I'm putting my chef skills to the test today. Sort of. It's not a complicated meal, per se, but I haven't made lemon chicken over spaghetti in a long time and I'm doing my best to recall Gramma Jean's recipe from memory.

That's how she cooks, too. There's not a single recipe card in her house, but she's the best cook I know. My dad never took an interest in his mother's skills, but I did. I didn't have a choice. When my mom and dad got divorced and I begged to stay with my dad, she was the one who raised me. She was the one who was there while Dad logged long hours at work, and she'd force me to sit at the kitchen table and do my homework while she started dinner. She'd hum while she cooked, and she'd make up words to the melodies of familiar songs but she'd change the words to whatever she was cooking. I distinctly remember "Chicken, ah lemon chicken" sung to the Archies' old song, "Sugar Sugar."

I hum the song while I slice open the fresh lemons—a requirement of this recipe, as Gramma Jean would say. The bottled lemon juice just doesn't taste the same, and she's right. I've tried it both ways. Fresh is always the way to go.

I haven't exactly invited Kaylee over for dinner yet, but since we're seeing each other now, I assume she'll be over at some point.

I decide to send her a text just to make sure.

Me: *Are you coming over tonight?*

Her reply comes quickly.

Peaches: *I'm at Ellie's now and I was planning to head home next.*

Me: *Care to detour here? I'll make it worth your time.* [eggplant emoji]

Peaches: *Again?*

Me: *I can't seem to get enough.* [lemon emoji] [spaghetti emoji]

Peaches: *I'm not sure what that means, but I'm interested.* [purple devil emoji]

Me: *LOL. I'm cooking dinner. Trying to show off my talents for you.*

Peaches: *What time are we eating?*

Me: *Should be ready around six.*

Peaches: *I'll be there in a half hour. I have something to tell you, too.*

I'm nervous about what that means, but I'm doing my best to trust her.

Me: *See you soon.*

I hum my way through the entire recipe as I realize how smart it was of Gramma Jean to make up the words to songs. Who needs recipe cards when you can sing your way through it?

Kaylee shows up a half hour later just as she said she would, and she's looking all naughty schoolteacher in a skirt and blouse that would look much better on my floor than where they currently reside.

I sigh as I look at her. Jesus, she's pretty.

I note the photographer across the street and I greet her with a kiss before I slam the door shut behind her. My hand moves up to her neck as I pull her in a little closer, this kiss just for us versus the way it started for the media.

She pulls back, and I feel…rejected.

It's stupid to feel that way, I know. But it's there.

She's a little breathless as her chest heaves up and down.

"Everything okay?"

She shrugs. "Not really."

"Come on in," I say, waving her toward the kitchen. My chest suddenly feels heavy. I try to ignore it along with the ominous mood in the room, but it's like a wave I can't escape.

I resume my work as I nod toward a stool at the counter where she can watch me work and we can chat. The water is boiling, so I grab the bag of noodles. "What's going on?" I ask, tearing it open and pouring the noodles into the water.

"My ex showed up at school today." She blurts the words so fast I almost miss them. "Oh, and he wants me back."

My stomach twists violently. I pull a little too hard and break the bag in half, and I nearly drop the plastic in the water as noodles fly all over the stovetop. "What?" I ask as I attempt to clean up my mess.

I'm not a messy chef, I swear.

I turn around and face her. "Your ex, like the guy you said was the only guy you ever loved? Or a different one?" *Please say a different one.*

"Yep. That's the one."

"He just showed up out of the blue," I say flatly.

She presses her lips together and nods. "Yep. And he's offering me everything I wanted back when we were together. The whole reason I ended things with him was because he didn't want kids. And now…well, I guess he does."

"Do you *want* to get back together with him?" I ask carefully as I ignore the nerves currently lighting up my chest.

I *literally* just realized I'm falling for this girl and decided it was safer not to tell her because I don't know how she feels. We keep saying this is just casual.

What if I missed my window?

"I don't know what I want," she mutters as she stares down at the counter. Her eyes won't meet mine, and I'm pretty sure that's my answer. She wants to get back together with the loser.

Maybe that's not fair. Maybe he's a perfectly nice guy. But if she ditches me for him, in my head…he'll forever be a loser.

"What did Ellie say?" I ask since she just came from there and if I know her the way I think I do, surely she discussed this issue with her sister-in-law.

"She asked me the same thing you did and I gave her the same answer." She finally glances up at me, and when her eyes connect with mine, I see the pain and indecision there. "I told him you and I were pretty serious."

"Thank you," I say softly. "Thanks for protecting what we're doing. But I never intended to take anything away from you with this whole thing. You deserve to be happy. You deserve so much, and if you want to be with him…" I trail off.

Don't be with him.

Stay with me.

Give me time to work this out.

Give me time to gain the courage to admit how I feel. I've never done it before, and I don't know how it works.

Give me time to stick this out…because I'm afraid this first little bump in the road will only cause a divide between us and the things that were in our grasp will just fall away with the sunset.

"He wants to take me to dinner," she says softly. "He's in town until Sunday, and I didn't know if it's okay to do that given our…situation."

"If you want to go to dinner with him, go to dinner with him." But please don't go to dinner with him.

I wish I could make myself say those words.

They won't form on my tongue, though. Instead, the thoughts I had just last night that I don't want to leave anything on the table when it comes to her seem to flutter away in the breeze as a different sort of feeling takes over.

I don't want to take a chance away—her *future* away—from her. I don't know what he's offering her. If she wants to explore things with him, I don't want to stand in her way…not when I'm so unsure of what I could really offer her.

Not if he's the right one for her.

I wish it could be me…but I'm just not sure it is.

CHAPTER 15

Kaylee

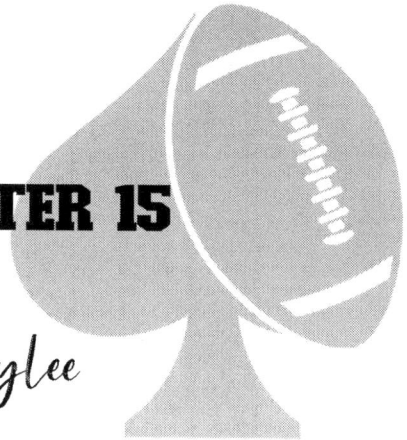

I wish he'd just tell me not to go to dinner with Dane. My gut is screaming at me that he wants to say it, but something's stopping him.

Instead, he told me to go. He told me he doesn't want to hold me back from the things I deserve.

Further evidence that he doesn't want whatever it is that I do want. Further proof that his words about keeping things casual between us are one hundred percent sincere.

Just when it felt like he was starting to let me in, he's pushing me away.

When I first got to his house and he pulled me into his arms and kissed me the way he did, my choice was clear. As much as I once loved Dane, what I feel for Ben is completely different. Dane was there when I needed someone the most, but he's my past. Ben is my future.

Or at least I was starting to hope he was. Now I'm not so sure.

He's quiet while we eat. Too quiet. Clearly he's struggling with what I just confessed, and I'm not sure how to bring things back to the way they were before. I want to lighten the mood, but we're in this unfamiliar territory I can't seem to navigate my way around.

I try to make conversation.

"How was your day?" I ask as I twirl some noodles around my fork.

"Fine." He avoids eye contact with me.

"What did you do?"

"Workouts."

A few beats of silence pass and the only noise in the room is chewing. "This is fantastic. Did your grandma teach you the recipe?"

"Yeah." He doesn't look up from his plate with his one-word answer and he doesn't acknowledge the compliment.

"What's your favorite recipe of hers?" I ask. I'm grasping at straws here.

"Pulled pork." It's the first two word answer I've gotten since we sat to eat.

I try to come up with some open-ended questions to ask, things to get him talking again, but it's like he closed the shutters. "Tell me about your grandma."

"She's my dad's mom. She still lives in Montana."

I wait a few beats for him to add something—*anything*—but he doesn't. I clear my throat. "Will you see her while you're up there?"

He nods.

My fork scrapes against the plate, and the screeching noise is actually a comfort amid the noodle chewing.

I sigh loudly as I set my fork down. "Is everything okay?"

He finally glances up from his plate. He shrugs. "Yeah. Fine."

So that's how it's going to be. He's just going to shut down. The fact that he's not going to bother fighting for whatever we seemed to be starting speaks volumes. I guess I was feeling something he wasn't, and it's better to learn that now than to keep pining for something that just isn't going to happen.

"Doesn't seem fine, but okay," I mutter.

I don't really know where we go from here. We eat the rest of our meal in silence because I'm tired of trying to carry the conversation. Once dinner is done and the dishes are clean—something we work on together even though we didn't actually talk about who would be doing the dishes and it just seemed to come naturally—I press my lips together.

"I guess I'll head home." I expect him to try to stop me or at the very least to kiss me or make some sexual joke or to say *something.*

He doesn't. He simply nods.

And in doing so, he's telling me to leave without saying the words. He's telling me he doesn't want me here. He's telling me I'd be better off with someone who wants me back—with someone who I have a history with, someone closer to my age who wants the same sort of future I want even though less than two hours ago, I didn't know he wanted that same future and I hadn't thought about him in quite a while.

And so I go. No goodbye kiss—not even for the benefit of the man in the car parked across the street eager to get a photo of whoever's walking out of Ben Olson's house.

I'm beyond confused as I get into my BMW. Is our deal even still on? Are *any* of our deals still on? There's the secret sex, the fake relationship, the pretending in front of my family…and then there's the real feelings that were blossoming so quickly that I feel sucker punched as I start the car.

My chest is heavy and heat pricks behind my eyes.

We were just having some fun, right?

So then why does this feel like rejection? Why does it hurt so damn bad?

And why do I wish he'd come running after me to stop me from leaving to tell me he feels it, too?

I trudge through my evening as I debate whether I should call Dane while I wait for some communication from Ben to come through.

My phone is silent, though. As silent as he was all through dinner.

I think about calling Ellie or chatting with Kate about this, but I'm afraid I'll get emotional, and when I get emotional, my gums start to flap. And if my gums start to flap, I might confess how hard and how quickly I've fallen for Ben Olson (and his Big O Thunder). I might give away the secret we've fought so hard to keep.

And now, more than ever, I can't afford for my family to find out. If it's over before they ever even knew about it, that's fine. Nothing has to change. But once the word is out, relationships are at stake. If Jack knows Ben hurt me by completely giving up on me out of the blue rather than fighting through our first obstacle together, he'd choose to protect me over his friend. And who knows what that could translate to in the locker room or on the field.

I certainly don't want to be the cause of that sort of unnecessary drama.

I'll give him the night to think all this through. Tomorrow's a new day.

I say the words in my head as a little pep talk, but it doesn't work. I ward off the tears until I'm by myself in my bedroom at Jack's house, and then I cry as devastation rolls through me that I might've missed my chance with Ben.

CHAPTER 16

Kaylee

Me: Are you free for dinner?

I text Dane while I'm on my lunch break. I don't know where he is or what he's doing, but I do know that I have a small window to figure out whether the spark is still there between us before he heads back to Chicago.

Dane: I was hoping you'd ask me that. Yes I am.

I'd invite him over, but I don't really want to. Jack is such a presence and while Dane and Jack have met before, I don't really want this dinner to be about anything other than whatever it is Dane wants to talk about.

Me: Great. Choose a restaurant at your hotel and I'll meet you there at seven.

He sends back a thumbs up emoji.

A freaking thumbs up.

It's such a freaking passive aggressive response to anything.

Use your words, Dane. Especially with a language arts teacher.

Was he always like that? I'm having a hard time remembering, but maybe it's because the guy I've most recently been bedding uses dirty emojis instead. A thumbs up from Ben would probably be next to a peach to indicate that he's planning to stick his thumb in my ass.

Why does that thought make me squirm a little?

I shake it off.

I stay a little later than usual at work as I start packing up my classroom. We only have seven school days remaining, and that means only seven school days left for me to clean out my room since I won't be returning.

When I pull into the driveway, I spot Ben's Scout. My heart races. He's here! He came to see me!

And then I head inside, where reality plows into me as I realize they're out back in Jack's workout man cave shed.

It's time to get ready for my dinner, so I change out of my work clothes and into a dress that's more on the casual side than the sexy side, and I slip out the front door before anybody sees me.

Regret pulses in my chest for the entire drive as I make my way toward Dane's hotel. I should've at least gone out to say hello. Instead, I snuck out for a date with another man.

It all feels so wrong.

I realize on the drive over that meeting at the hotel was a bad idea. I may be sending the wrong message as Dane will certainly think I'm just making it easy for him to invite me up to his room, but that will definitely not be happening. I have an image to portray, after all, even after the weirdness of yesterday's dinner. Even after the fact that I haven't heard from Ben all day.

I valet my car then head inside to the restaurant Dane sent in a follow up text after the thumbs up. I spot him standing outside the restaurant. He's clean-shaven in his khaki pants and a polo shirt, clearly fresh from today's conference, and he's handsome as he stands there.

He's not the bad boy Ben is. He doesn't crush beer cans on his forehead, and the only time he visits strip clubs is with his girlfriend's permission when he and his buddies are attending a bachelor party. He's smart and loyal, dedicated to learning and working. He cared about good grades through high school and college and worked hard to achieve them. He's warm and friendly, the kind of guy who can strike up a conversation with anybody and yet he's stubborn enough to fight for what he really wants.

Even his hair is gelled back neatly.

He's perfect on paper.

But perfect on paper doesn't really translate the same as perfect for me.

Ben's certainly not perfect for me, either, yet I can't seem to stop thinking about him. His eyes as they follow my movements. The way his mouth tastes. His clean, fresh scent. The way he makes me laugh. The way he makes me feel like the only person in the room even though everyone is there to see him.

But he doesn't want me the way I want him.

I'm so confused. I have no idea where my feelings stand for Dane. I suppose that's why I showed up here tonight.

His eyes follow me in. If Ben were standing there, he'd have his leg kicked up against the wall while he leaned back on it, and he'd be staring down at his phone. He'd glance up at me and heat would pass between us once our eyes connected. He'd shoot me that panty melting grin, and he'd have his hand up my skirt under the table before we even placed our drink order.

On the other hand, Dane stands patiently waiting for me, a smile tipping the corners of his lips as he eyes me until I stop in front of him. He leans in and gently kisses my cheek— probably the most risqué form of PDA I'll see tonight out of him.

I'm not sure which I prefer. One's racy and exciting and thrilling, and the other is comforting and kind and sweet.

Racy and exciting doesn't work in the long term, though. Kind and sweet have a better shot.

"Let's go on in," he says, and he takes charge as he tells the hostess we need a table for two. We're led to a quiet, romantic booth along the wall, and it's sort of nice being out with someone the media at large gives zero fucks about. I don't think I'm a recognizable enough face yet to be splashed all over the gossip sites tomorrow, but I guess time will tell.

I study the menu mostly because I don't really know what to say. I looked at it earlier and already decided on a shrimp dish.

Dane sets his menu down first, and I glance up at him.

"Thank you for agreeing to dinner," he says softly.

I offer a short smile and nod as I return my gaze to the menu.

"You already know what you're getting," he guesses, and my lips tip up into a more genuine smile. "If I still know you the way I think I do, you studied the menu earlier today and already made your decision."

I lift a shoulder as I give a little laugh. "Maybe."

"So why are you hiding?"

I set the menu down. "This is all just…" I flail for the words for a beat, and then they come to me. "It's so out of the blue, Dane. I moved on. I had to. I was sad when I knew it wouldn't work out in the long term for the two of us, and it took me some time to get over losing you. You were the only man I ever dated who didn't care who my brothers were, and that's still true."

Except for Ben.

"You don't date football players," he points out. "Something strange is going on."

I sigh. I forgot how well he knows me. "Nothing strange is going on. That became my mantra because I was tired of being used by boys who were trying to get to Jack and Luke through me. But Ben doesn't need to use people to get to the top. He got there all by himself."

"But Olson?" he says, narrowing his eyes as he twists his lips. "He's a party guy, Kay. You deserve more than that."

I press my lips together as a certain rage seems to pass through my chest. The feeling is so strong that it momentarily knocks the wind out of me. I clear my throat. "I will not sit here and allow you to talk about someone you know nothing about. He is a wonderful, kind, amazing man." *A wonderful, kind, amazing man who fucks like a beast.* "And he puts me first. He cares about my wants and my needs." *In bed.* "He's funny and he constantly surprises me." *When he fingers me under the table.*

But it's not just the sexual stuff. Yes, that's the forefront of our relationship because that's our deal. But in becoming intimately close with him, I've also gotten to know who he is as a person. And while the sex caught my attention, the man himself is the reason I've stuck around.

"So you're in love with him." He says the words flatly even though I think there's a question in them.

"Yes." I am. Yes, of course that's what it is. I knew I was falling, and I knew I was in dangerous waters, but this is the first time I've admitted it even to myself.

I'm no longer falling. I'm there. I fell, and I can't get up.

I am in love with Ben Olson…a man who doesn't do real relationships.

I am so fucked.

CHAPTER 17

Kaylee

My mind continues to center on Ben as we order our meals and the waitress drops off some rolls. I grab one and slather on some butter before I scarf it down, carb counting be damned.

I'm nervous eating. I know it doesn't make any sense, that usually when tummies are full of nerves it makes normal people *not* want to eat, but I'm the opposite. When I'm stressed or nervous, my body demands carb overload.

I should've ordered pasta. Maybe I'll get the chocolate cake for dessert.

"What are you nervous about?" Dane asks, and the way he asks it makes me think he's dropping a hint at something.

I can't exactly admit that I'm nervous where I stand with Ben right now. I can't exactly tell him that I've fallen for a guy who doesn't believe in marriage when that's a huge part of the future I always dreamed of.

"I'm not nervous. Just hungry. Lunch was at eleven and I haven't had time to grab anything since."

"Tell me about your first year of teaching," he says. He's trying to make conversation, and I'm sure he's going to point out all the places where he could so easily slip back into my life, and I don't want to be here.

At all.

I want to be at Ben's place. I want to be snuggled in his arms on his couch while we watch a game or a movie or just talk. I want to be in that afterglow when he's thoroughly worked my body over.

Instead I'm sitting at a table across from my ex.

"It sucked and I'm not going back."

His brows rise. "You're not? I thought teaching was what you wanted?"

"It took me a little bit of time to realize teaching was what my *dad* wanted for me. But he also wanted me to be happy, and I didn't find that in my first career."

"What are you going to do?" he asks.

I lift a shoulder. "My sister-in-law does public relations, and I'm going to work part time for her. She's going to set me up with some paid sponsorships."

His brows knit together. "You're going to be an influencer?"

I shrug. "If people are interested. Ellie seems to think I have a great angle being related to not one but two football players."

"And dating a third," he says.

I nod.

"Weren't you trying your whole life to get away from all that?"

"Yep. But it was Ben who made me see how much sense it makes to lean into the gifts I've been given rather than trying so hard to run away from them." I shrug. "I think what it comes down to is I always felt like I was last in line in my own family. I spent so much time trying to stand out to my dad that I chose the career he wanted for me rather than the one I wanted for myself."

"What's the one you want for yourself?"

"I don't know," I murmur. "Working with kids in a different aspect. I want to focus on health and fitness, on getting kids out to play instead of staying inside with electronics. I'm working on a proposal for a kids' fitness program. I have a lot of research to do and I'm going to start hitting that once the school year is over."

"So you have plans."

I nod. "Yeah. If you're asking whether I'm staying here or coming back home…"

He raises his brows. Yep, that's exactly what he was asking.

I take a sip of wine. "The answer is simple. This is home now."

It doesn't feel like it most days, but I'm already lying about everything else. Why not add one more on top? Hopefully it'll encourage him to back down. He'll go back home to Chicago and the onslaught of confusion he has incited will die away in a few days.

He opens his mouth to say something, but then he seems to think twice about it. He presses his lips together. "I'm glad you've found your home."

Our meals arrive, and I ask a little about his work conference to get the heat off me. He's a big data engineer with a computer science degree, and the conference he's attending is all about interpreting statistics. He's passionate as he talks about it, but I'm pretty sure my eyes glazed over the second I asked the first question.

He finishes his last bite and uses his napkin to wipe his mouth before he throws it on top of his plate. "My boss thinks I should get a Master's degree in business data analytics to help me advance my career."

"Oh?" I ask. "Do they have that program near you?" I've hardly touched my shrimp, but I seem to have lost my appetite.

He nods. "It's a pretty common degree these days, but my life is pretty much already dedicated to work." He glances up from his plate to meet my eyes. "I think I *had* to throw myself into it since I was nursing a broken heart."

He holds the eye contact, and I glance away first.

"We both knew there was an expiration date," I say softly.

"Did we?" he asks. "Or were we just two people who weren't quite ready yet?"

I blow out a breath. "No," I say, shaking my head. "We were two people who weren't right for each other."

"But we find ourselves in a different place now." He takes a sip of his wine, too, and the thought strikes me that I don't see Ben ordering wine at a restaurant. It doesn't matter who drinks what...the point is just how vastly different these two men are.

"Yeah, we do. I'm in Vegas. You're in Chicago now." I know he doesn't mean geographically, but my mental energy of fighting him off is starting to wear thin.

He nods thoughtfully. "Yeah," he murmurs.

"It's getting late, and I have work tomorrow," I say once he's paid the bill. It's not that late—not even nine o'clock yet—but a part of me wants to get home to see if Ben is still there. I stand, and he follows suit.

He sets a hand on my lower back to guide me. A year ago, that would've melted me. Today, I wish it were Ben's hand.

"I'll walk you to your car," he says.

I hold up a hand. "That's not necessary. I valeted anyway."

"Then I'll wait with you."

I press my lips together. Obviously he wants the extra few minutes, and I decide not to fight it.

I hand my ticket off to the valet, and it's fairly empty so it shouldn't be too long of a wait.

"Thanks for meeting me," Dane says. He grabs my hand and squeezes it.

"It was nice to catch up," I say politely.

He nods and looks down at me, and I see the familiar question in his eyes. When you've been with someone long enough, you can easily ascertain what they want just from a single look, and his eyes are telling me he wants to take me upstairs and do the things we did once upon a time. His eyes flick to my lips, and that's when his hand comes up around my neck and he leans in for a quick peck on the lips.

It's so fast I don't even realize it's happening. A little spark ignites in my chest. It's not an inferno of need or a wave of desire, but it's home. It's comfort. It's familiar. And we *did* have an awful lot of good times together. We did laugh together. We did have some amazing sex.

Ahem…the *second* best sex of my life.

Still, though, my first thought as he pulls back is that I'm worried someone will see, that someone just took a picture and this whole Ben thing is going to blow up tomorrow as further evidence is planted that what we're doing isn't real. I take a quick glance around, and I don't see any photographers. That doesn't mean there aren't any, though.

Regardless of who might've caught that or not, as far as Dane knows, I have a boyfriend. I back out of his orbit, and he has the audacity to look a little hurt by that.

"I have a boyfriend," I say quietly.

"It was just a friendly kiss," he protests. "I didn't mean anything by it."

"You were trying to make me see whether the spark between us is still there."

"Well?" he asks pointedly.

"It doesn't matter. I'm in love with somebody else. I'm happy you've realized what you want out of life, Dane, but it can't be with me."

"Can't it?" He shrugs. "I'm in love with you, and I know you still feel it. Just think about what a life with someone like him might be like, and think about our history together. When it was good between us, it was *good*. We can have all that back if you'll just give us a chance."

A white BMW pulls up, and that's me. "I need to go. Enjoy the rest of your time here in Vegas. Have a safe trip back home."

I rush into the driver's seat and don't bother looking back, but I know he watches me until my car is out of sight.

CHAPTER 18

Ben

I went hard today.

Too hard.

My body feels like Jell-O and I'm a fucking idiot.

I flick off the television since I can't pay attention to it right now anyway. I'm lying across the couch staring at a blank screen.

I'm antsy, but my body's too worn down to move.

She's probably on a date with that douchebag right now and I'm too nervous to call and find out for sure.

I went to Jack's place with the hope of running into her. I'm always at his place, so it's not like it was out of the ordinary, but I never saw her. Maybe she's happier that way. Who knows? But I owe it to her to explore that. I can't make the sorts of promises for the things she wants, and so my easiest out was to run.

Nights like this make me want to go out, get fuck drunk, and make a complete ass of myself. Instead, I'm stuck at home playing the role of somebody else while I do my best to make my boss happy.

And maybe my biggest problem right now is that I have nobody to talk to about my current situation. My closest friends are related to the center of the issue, and I don't trust anybody outside of that circle except my dad, who's currently two days away from taking this girl's *mother* on a date, and Gramma Jean.

I snap my fingers. That's it! I'll call Gramma Jean. She'll know what to do. Or she'll give me a new recipe to try. Either way, hearing her voice will be a win. I glance at the clock. It's a little before nine o'clock her time, so she might be asleep, but I dial her number anyway.

"Benny Boy!" she answers, and my chest warms hearing her voice. There's nobody like grandma.

"Hey Gramma. How have you been?"

"Benjamin Joseph Olson, why has it been so long since you've called me?" she asks—the same thing she asks every time I call.

"I'm sorry."

"Aside from wondering what you've been up to, I've been just fine, sugar."

"Did I wake you?" I ask.

"Nah. My show's on."

I huff out a chuckle. "Sorry."

"I hear it in your voice. What's the matter? Is it a girl?"

God, she knows me well. "Something like that."

"Oh, Benny. What did you do now?"

"I didn't do anything," I protest.

"And in doing nothing, that caused problems?" she correctly guesses.

"Maybe."

"You never call me out of the blue at nine o'clock on a Wednesday night. You call me on Tuesday late morning when you remember. Now cut to the chase, kid. MacGyver just went to commercial and when it comes back, I have to find out how he solves this problem."

I laugh, and it's the first genuine laugh I've felt since Kaylee left my place yesterday. Only Gramma would not realize she could pause live television so she doesn't have to miss a beat—or better yet, stream her program. She's had a crush on that MacGyver guy as long as I've been alive.

"Click pause, Gramma," I say patiently. I'm met with confused silence, so I add, "On your television remote. You can pause it so you don't miss your show."

"I will not pause Richard Dean Anderson." Her tone is serious, and I can just picture her face as her eyes flash with anger at my suggestion.

"Okay, okay," I relent with another laugh. "There's a girl that I have feelings for but she's the little sister of one of my best friends. It's complicated, and now I'm pretty sure she's on a date with another guy."

"You're the better man. She will choose you. Can I get back to my show now?"

I blow out a frustrated breath even though I know she's just teasing me. "Gramma, you've seen that show twenty-five thousand times."

"You know I'm teasing you, sugar. Why is she on a date with another guy?"

I stare at the blank television screen in front of me. "They used to date. He showed up out of nowhere saying he wanted to give her the future she always wanted. Marriage, kids, the whole shebang, and I've never wanted that future so I can't make those same promises."

"But she's been with you anyway?"

"Yeah. We're sort of seeing each other on the sly." And by seeing each other, I mean fucking. But I can't tell Gramma that, obviously.

"On the sly from who?" she asks.

I clear my throat. "Her family. Specifically her brother who's my buddy. And now we have a deal where we're publicly dating so the media catches wind that I'm not the partying asshole I've been made out to be."

She's quiet a beat, and then she says, "That's a lot to process. Let me get this straight. What I'm hearing is you're lying to the media, lying to her family, lying to her, and lying to yourself?"

"How am I lying to her?"

"By not telling her how you feel. And before you ask me how you're lying to yourself," she interrupts as I begin to protest, "clearly you're in love with her and you won't admit it."

I sputter some nonsensical noises, but she's right. All it took was one conversation for her to nail the issue.

"Listen up, kid, because I'm about to drop some wisdom on you," she says, and I chuckle. This right here? This is the entire reason I called her. "First, falling in love and being with someone doesn't necessarily mean you have to marry them. Are you absolutely sure that's what she wants? Or do you think maybe she just wants *you*? And on the other hand, just because marriage didn't work out for your mother and father doesn't mean it won't work out for you. You're a stubborn boy, and once you latch onto a belief, there's no swaying you from it. But think about your life with this girl, and then think of your life without it. What are you willing to sacrifice for her on either side of that line?"

I clear my throat. "I made her your lemon chicken."

She huffs out a soft laugh. "Chicken, ah lemon chicken," she sings.

"I remembered the whole song. And she liked the chicken, too."

"I've got a new one for you." She clears her throat and starts a new song to the tune of "Rock Around the Clock." "We're gonna cook around the stove tonight, we're gonna cook cook cook some tasty bites."

I laugh. "You're the best, Gramma."

"Right back at you, kiddo. Now keep the calls to the morning when MacGyver isn't on."

"When I'm up there for the summer, I'm getting you a streaming service and training you how to use it so you can watch your show any time of the day or night."

"Sounds good, sugar," she says, and I can hear the smile in her voice. "Keep me updated on the girl."

"Will do." I hang up, and while that conversation didn't solve any problems, it did give me a whole lot of food for thought.

Life with Kaylee versus life without her. I know what I want, but that doesn't mean I'm willing to sacrifice my entire belief system. But I think it *is* worth a conversation. It might end up being a difficult conversation, or one where the outcome isn't what I want, but at least then I'll have answers versus sitting in this land of total confusion.

Now if I could just get "Cook around the Stove" out of my head, I'll be all set.

CHAPTER 19

Kaylee

The final bell rings and it's official. I have one week of school left. Forever and ever.

Amen.

I tell my students I'll see them tomorrow as they file out of the room, and then I collapse into my chair once the hinged door latches shut behind the last kid.

I blow out a breath. All the papers have been graded and returned. We're prepping for final exams. Our principal thinks it's important preparation for high school to give these types of exams, and we're required to make them worth ten percent of students' grades. Janet has told me that we should prepare students by giving them a chance to learn study skills in class as we study for the exam together.

It's actually a nice break from the grind of teaching literature all year. Read a book, discuss it, write an essay on it. Rinse, repeat. We've hit all the standards we need to hit, and I feel like my students are well prepared for the exam. Still, though, doing exam prep for a week gives me plenty of time to pack up and prepare for whatever comes next.

The door opens a half hour or so after the last bell and Ashley walks in. We're not besties, but we've become work friends. "So is it true?"

My brows dip. "Is what true?"

"You and the Big O Thunder."

I laugh. "Yeah. It's true."

"Oh my God, girl! How could you not tell me?"

I lift a shoulder. "It's kind of new and I wasn't ready to talk about it yet."

"How's it going?" She plops on top of one of the student desks.

I sigh. Not great at the moment considering we're getting close to forty-eight hours of silence, but I don't mention that. Instead, I offer a smile as I'm suddenly thankful that we're nothing more than work friends. She can't tell my fake smiles from my genuine ones. "It's going amazingly well."

"I'm happy for you. I heard you're not coming back. Is it because of him?"

I press my lips together. "It's all part of it, I think. I can't just live my life because of who my brothers are. I never thought it would matter, but literally every day I get comments from kids about my brothers or my boyfriend. Janet hates me because she's a Seahawks fan. It's been a tough year."

"Yeah, the first year is never easy, but add on top of it all that stuff and I'm sure it would drive most anyone away." She glances around. "You need any help packing up?"

I shake my head. "It won't take long. Do you want my teaching materials? I'm not going to need them anymore."

She nods enthusiastically. "I'll take anything you want to share."

I turn around and grab a few binders off the bookcase behind my desk and walk them over to her. "We can start with these, and I'll send kids over with more."

"Amazing. Thank you so much!" She flips through the pages. "This stuff is so good. Are you sure you don't want to teach anymore?"

I shrug. "I just don't think it's for me."

"So what are you going to do?" she asks.

"I'm working on it."

The door opens again, and we both turn to look at who's coming in.

And if *I* am surprised at who walks in, Ashley is freaking shocked.

"Oh my God. It's really you!" Ashley squeals as the man wearing a backward baseball cap walks into my room.

His dark eyes connect with mine.

My thighs clench together.

"I am such a huge fan!" Ashley continues to squeal.

Ben nods and offers a smile. "Thank you."

"So this really is real?" she asks.

I look at him and shrug. We haven't spoken in two days since the weird dinner at his house, but he's here now my first thought is that he's here to end this whole charade.

"Yeah," he says. He glances out the window and I'm not sure how to get rid of Ashley so I can find out what Ben is doing here. He finally returns his gaze to me and takes care of that particular issue. "Can we talk?"

I nod and look at Ashley. "I'm sorry. Would you mind excusing us?"

"Of course." She gives Ben a wide smile. "Knock 'em dead this season." She winks at me. "I'll lock the door on my way out." She must be oblivious to the tension in the room, or maybe she thinks it's of the *sexual* brand, but either way, she goes.

And she does lock the door.

"What's up, Trouble?" I ask. It's weird having him here in this classroom. He's such a huge presence at somewhere around six and a half feet tall built completely out of muscle, and he looks absolutely out of place as he looks around for somewhere to sit. The desks in my classroom have the seats attached, so it's unlikely he'll be able to fold his legs into one of those. Instead, he wanders over toward the window and sighs.

"You went to dinner with him?"

I hear the vulnerability in his voice.

I clear my throat as I wonder how he knows. Did a photo emerge? Was it of that quick kiss at the end of our date? "Yes."

"Did you kiss him?"

"He kissed me."

He turns toward me and presses his lips together for a beat. "Do you want him back?"

I shrug, not sure how much of my own vulnerability to allow through here. "I don't know. We have a history, and he's telling me all the things I want to hear, but I've got a contract for the next few months with you and I won't do anything to jeopardize that."

He nods as he focuses his gaze down at the ground. "A contract. Right. Look, if you want to be with him, if he's your future, I won't stand in your way."

"Why do you keep pushing me toward him?" The words tumble unfiltered out of my mouth, and even I'm surprised for a second that I actually said them…but I don't regret it.

His eyes move slowly up to mine. "I'm not trying to push you. I'm doing everything I can to give you the space to make your choice."

"What are my choices, Ben?" I ask. Frustration strangles me and I can't help that it's evident in my voice.

He lifts a shoulder. "Going back to him or sticking this thing out with me."

"That's it?" I press. It just feels like there's more he's not saying, and I'm not sure how hard to push to get him to talk.

"Is that why you came here today? To ask if I'm going back to him?"

He blows out a long breath but doesn't say anything.

I try another tack. "I haven't heard from you in two days. You were weird at dinner the other night the second I mentioned Dane, and you're being weird now."

"I'm sorry," he says quietly. This isn't him. This man in front of me…it's not the playful, fun, sexy Ben I've come to know. Something is weighing him down. "This is just unfamiliar to me."

"What is?"

He licks his lips and glances out the window before his eyes return to the spot on the floor in front of him. He sighs again, and I brace myself for whatever he's about to tell me. "It's just…it's everything."

"Define everything." I fold my arms over my chest as nerves take hold of my heart.

He turns to the window, like he can't look at me while he makes this confession, and I'm suddenly less anxious and more scared of whatever's weighing on him.

"Come on, Ben," I practically yell. "Just say what you want."

"I want you all to myself," he begins. "I want you for more than just one night. I want you to tell that douchebag it's over with him rather than being confused with whether you want to be with him or continue this charade that's not really a charade at all anymore with me." He finally turns around and his eyes connect with mine. They're full of need and want and…something warm. Is it…love?

He lowers his voice. "I want you to tell me you want me, too, that you're feeling these same things, this same confusion and this feeling like you can't imagine life without me in it now because that's how I feel about you."

He walks a few steps closer to me and he slaps his palm on my desk. "And I want to perch you on the edge of this desk so I can slam my cock into you because however many days it's been is way too fucking long for me to go without being inside you." His eyes burn into mine. "There. That's what I want. Happy now?"

I push my chair back from my desk as conflicting feelings plow into me. "No, I'm not *happy* now." I stand up and place my palms on my desk. I lean on them in some attempt to look intimidating—but I'm no match for him. "You don't get to come here and throw out all these confusing words and act like *I* am the one causing the problems between us."

His eyes flash with confusion as I straighten.

"You don't get to stand there and pretend like I'm the one holding us back." My voice is a hiss. As much as his words pulsed a sense of relief in me, they also incited a bit of anger…and apparently anger is winning at the moment.

"No, I don't want Dane," I say. I clench my fists and my voice starts to rise as the anger seems to take flight. "I want *you*. I'm falling for you, Ben, and that's fucking terrifying since you've been nothing but honest about what you want from me."

"I lied," he hisses back, and he places his palms on my desk in a face-off with me.

I flinch at his words then mirror his position as I lean down on my palms again. "About what?"

"About what I want. Because fuck it all, I'm falling for you, too. I can't give you the things you want in your future, the things you *deserve*, and *that* is why I haven't told you how I feel."

We stare each other down, and I can't tell if we're angry at each other or what the hell is going on.

The air is thick with tension, and as his eyes burn into mine, something snaps.

We want the same damn thing.

We want different futures, but we want each other.

The whole reason I ended my last relationship was because I wanted the future he didn't want...and now it's happening again.

Still, though...isn't it worth giving it a try? Maybe I don't need the things I always dreamed of if I have Ben. Maybe he's the ultimate dream.

If nothing else, we've got at least the next five months to figure it out.

CHAPTER 20

Ben

"So we both want the same thing?" I finally ask as I straighten to a full stand.

Her brows that were arched in anger smooth over as she straightens, too. "Um…yeah? I think maybe we do. For the next five months, anyway."

"To be clear since this is not my forte, I want to be with you, and you want to be with me. I am falling for you and you are falling for me. Our dating for the media deal is still on even though we're sort of moving this to *actually* dating, we're still keeping our secret boning a secret, and I want to fuck you on your desk and you're giving me the green light to do so."

She looks up as she considers all that. "Yes." She nods. "Yes, yes, definitely yes, and a big fat *hell* yes."

I chuckle, and then I move around the desk to close the gap between us as my hand comes up to cup her neck. My thumb rests beside her throat, and I feel her pulse pick up speed as her eyes move up to mine. She doesn't just smell like sunshine. She looks like it, too. She's this calm in the storm my life has become. She's the lion tamer and the beast muzzler, the only one who I've ever let inside close enough to see my faults and who still wants me.

God *damn*, am I falling for her.

Something about the way she's looking up at me with all the vulnerability in the world as we both just made some pretty deep confessions makes me want to give her anything she wants.

I know I can't.

There are certain things I'm just not capable of, and we both know this.

But damn, as I look down into her eyes and see the need and hope in them...she certainly makes me want to try in a way nobody else ever has. Not even Tatum.

I crush my mouth to hers, and she links her arms around my neck as she opens her mouth to mine. Our tongues fight a war both sides are winning, and the primal urge to seal our words with action washes over me. It's a physical action that puts a stamp on the words we've spoken.

Neither of us said the *L* word, but we both talked around it. We're both on our way there. And now I'm going to show her how I feel in the language I know best.

I push her against her desk then lift her so her ass is perched on it, and then fuck taking it slow because I need to bury myself inside her.

She's wearing another glorious skirt, thank fuck, and I unzip my jeans and pull myself out. I stroke the monster a few times, and he's more than ready for her.

She catches her bottom lip between her teeth as she looks up at me, and she looks so innocent and pure perched there. I let out a low growl as I shove her panties to the side, line myself up, and shove my way in.

"Oh shit," I mutter as her pussy clings onto my cock for dear life.

And then I realize what's different.

I was so caught up in the moment that I didn't even think about a condom. "Oh shit," I say again, and my wide eyes come into focus on hers.

She shakes her head as lust wins. "It's fine. I'm on the pill."

"Thank God," I murmur, and then I shove into her a little harder.

She pushes her tits out as she leans back on her palms. She can't really move because of the position I have her in, but I drive into her over and over again. I move slowly, and it strikes me that this isn't just a quick fuck on her desk. It's something more.

Her eyes roll back in pleasure, and I thumb her clit from this angle while I shove my body into hers. She lets out one of her gorgeous little moans, and a hot fire detonates down my spine as my balls tighten up. Her pussy clenches a little tighter onto me, pushing me into an explosive climax as hot jets of come burst out of me and into her.

I never come inside a chick. Ever. Too many risks. Too many complications. Too much intimacy.

But holy hot damn does it feel *good*.

It's a million times better than regular sex, which is pretty damn awesome in the first place, and I don't think it's just because I went in bareback. I think it's because feelings are involved.

And *that* is real fucking scary.

But together…we can do this.

Before I pull out, I lean into her and cover her mouth with mine. We share a sensual, hot kiss as our tongues tangle lazily together as we each come down from those intense orgasms. I cup her neck in my palm, and her pulse beats wildly against my thumb. Holy *fuck* is it sexy.

I pull out of her and adjust her panties back into place. I tuck myself back into my pants before I move in a little closer and pull her into my arms. She's still sitting on the edge of her desk, and her cheek meets my torso as she clings to me and I to her.

"Well, I'll never look at this desk the same way again," she murmurs.

I chuckle as I tighten my arms around her and kiss the top of her head. "We should've done that weeks ago. Would've made work more bearable."

She presses a kiss to my stomach, and eventually I back away even though I don't want to. I'm sure she's ready to get out of here. It's been a taxing few minutes.

"You need any help packing this place up?" I ask as I glance around.

She nods. "I'll take any help I can get."

I head over to the wall where a bunch of posters and artwork hang almost all the way up to the ceiling. "Want me to take these down for you?"

"That would be a huge help." She hops off the desk and smooths her skirt before she sits in her chair and watches me. "I had to stand on a desk to get those up there."

I raise a brow. "Sounds dangerous."

"Oh, I'm sure if my department chair walked in, I would've been fired on the spot. Or at least cited for health and safety measures."

I reach up and pull down a poster, careful not to rip the corners. "You need me to have a talk with this department chair? She sounds like the devil."

She walks over and takes the poster from me. She pulls the staples out of the corners and sets them on a desk, and I go to work on the next one. "She basically is. Imagine if she walked in when you were just screwing me on my desk."

I laugh. "I bet she would've enjoyed the show. Sounds like she just needs a good fuck to loosen up a little."

She rolls her eyes. "She's a Seahawks fan."

I wrinkle my nose, which elicits a giggle. "Now I *really* want to meet her."

We're quiet as we work together as a team. I reach up to grab the high stuff then hand her the posters or student projects. If the staples came with them, she takes them out and makes piles of posters and work.

We're almost done with the first wall when she asks, "So just to reiterate…we're still keeping all this from my family, correct?"

I shrug. "It's your call, babe." I want her to make whatever decision makes her feel most comfortable. On the one hand, I don't want to hide what we have going. But on the other hand…I want to keep everything the way it is so we can navigate this new thing together and not worry about the additional pressures of her family's expectations of me or her or us together.

I just spent a whole lot of mental energy facing my feelings. If she wants to face her family next…I don't think I'm ready for that. I need some time. But I'd do it for her.

"I think we need to take it slow," she says, and her eyes dart a little nervously to mine. "We should know what we're doing before we bring other people into it. You know?"

I nod and move in to press a soft kiss to her lips as relief courses through my veins. "I agree. I just want to enjoy what we have. This way it's you and me against the world, and the only expectations pressuring us are the ones we place on this thing ourselves."

The nervousness seems to disappear from her eyes at my words. "Yes! That's exactly it. As much as I want to admit the truth to everyone, I'm not ready for their opinions. And they'll definitely have them. They always do."

I press my lips together as I grab the last poster and hand it to her.

"Thank you," she murmurs. She sets the staple in the pile with the rest then sweeps them into her palm. She heads toward the trash can with her pile. "Have you told anyone?"

I clear my throat. "Sort of. I mentioned a little bit of inner turmoil to my Gramma."

She turns around and walks slowly back toward me. "Your inner turmoil?"

I shrug. "I didn't want to stand in your way if you wanted to be with him." When she gets close enough, I pull her into my arms. "We have different visions of the future, and I know you want a husband and kids, something your ex is telling you he wants to give you when that's just never been what I wanted."

"He didn't want that, either, but he changed his mind..." she says, suggesting with the way she leaves the end of her sentence hanging that maybe I'll change my mind, too.

I think back to listening to my mom fight with my dad—the always stoic, unemotional Jeb who sat back and took her shit—before they got divorced. I was the kid pulled into the middle of it. My mom wanted me to live with her, and I wanted to live with my dad, and it was a constant struggle. Why would you do that to a kid?

I thought I was there with Tatum. But when shit hit the fan, the lesson reiterated was that women will always disappoint me with their lies. First my mom, then my ex. I learned that two people just aren't meant to be tied together for a lifetime, and I can't even imagine bringing a kid into that fold. It wouldn't be fair.

Maybe it works for other people, and that's fine. It's how the world keeps spinning, I guess. But I've been burned enough times to know it won't work for me.

"I won't," I say with finality.

She doesn't hide her disappointment, and even though we spent a few minutes in bliss, it already feels like there's an expiration date stamped on this relationship.

She wants kids and the dog and maybe a minivan and the white picket fence. I can provide a lot of the picture she once shared with me, but there's a big, gaping hole in the stuff I can't give her.

And as much as I wish I could be enough for her…I'm not sure I can.

CHAPTER 21

Kaylee

"We need to set up a photo shoot," Ellie says. She's sitting at her desk and she hasn't even greeted me with a *hello* yet as her gaze lands thoughtfully on me. "Your follows have shot up since Billy Peters posted that gossip piece on you and Ben. Have you been keeping an eye on it?"

I wave to Kate, who's sitting at her desk, and she smiles and waves back. I slide into the chair beside her so I can continue shadowing her as I shake my head. "Honestly I've been busy wrapping up the school year." And trying to figure out where Ben's head is at, which I leave out of the conversation.

"You started at one thousand twenty-four when you unlocked your account. Kate posted a few photos of you with your brothers, and people are biting. They want content with you and Ben, so that's why we need to set up a photo shoot."

I take my phone out of my pocket and open the app. I have over nine thousand followers. My jaw drops. "You did this?" I ask Kate. "In just a few days?"

She lifts a shoulder. "You toss up a couple pics each day, tag the right people, throw up the right hashtags, and voila."

"I've had some sponsors bite, but you don't get the really good offers until you have more followers," Ellie says. "Once you hit thirty thousand, you're considered an influencer and then there are strict advertising guidelines. You're off to a great start, but you get a pic of you and Ben up? It'll climb fast. I wonder if Ben was emailed any of the ones from that dinner the other night?"

I click my photos. "I have a couple selfies," I say. "They're not super professional or anything but they're sort of cute."

I flash my screen to Ellie, and she nods. "Send them to Kate. She can help with a caption and hashtags and scheduling. And as far as the interested sponsors, so far I've gotten offers from some leggings company, fitness gear, the team shop, teeth whiteners. Any of that sound up your alley?"

I tap a few buttons on my phone and text my photos to Kate. "Sure. I will gladly take whatever. Ben isn't comfortable with the engagement idea, but he green lighted dropping hints that we're heading that way. So if that's something you can work with, let me know."

"Oh absolutely," Ellie says. She jots down something on a pad of paper before looking up at me. "Between Nicki, Kate, and myself, I've got about a million vendors in my contacts. What sort of hints do you want to drop? I've got jewelry, bridal shops, salons, stylists, planners, bakeries…you name it. I can send out a few inquiries and see who sends back the best bids."

I nod. "Let's start there."

"Oh man," Ellie says, shaking her head. "This is going to drive people *wild* with curiosity." She grins.

My phone starts ringing. I glance at the screen, and I ignore the call with a heavy sigh.

"What's wrong?" Kate asks.

"My ex is in town. I went to dinner with him last night and I thought I was clear that I'm dating someone else, but now he's calling me again."

"Your ex?" Kate asks. "Dane?"

I nod. "He told me he wants kids and marriage and the whole nine yards now. Apparently he changed his mind and wants me back."

"Is that what you want?" she asks.

I shrug. "No. I mean, family, yes. Kids, marriage, a dog. All that, yeah. But I don't know if I want it with Dane anymore."

"Then who?" Ellie asks.

Ben. Ben freaking Olson. The Big O and his Big O Thunder.

I shrug instead of saying any of that. "I don't know, but I'm tied into a contract with Ben through September, so it doesn't really matter."

Kate pulls up the selfies I just sent her on her computer. "Too bad it would never work in reality with you and Ben. Look how freaking adorable you two are together."

I stiffen as I look at our genuine smiles on the screen in front of me. "Yeah. Guess we're pretty good actors, huh?" It's been an easy act to put on since it's not really an act at all…but also, I'm sort of stuck on her words about how it would never work out with Ben and me.

Why, exactly? Because Ben doesn't want those things? Because he's a decade older than me? Or is there something else she isn't saying?

"Well if you don't want what the ex wants, at least dropping these wedding hints on Instagram should get him to back off," Ellie says.

"I guess we'll see." I watch Kate as she posts one of the selfies to my Instagram account and tags Ben in the photo with just a red heart as the caption.

I've already gotten a handful of new followers since I looked a few minutes ago. I can't wait to see what sort of attention this selfie grabs.

* * *

I just got home to Jack's place when my phone rings again with another call from Dane. This time, I don't ignore it.

"Hey, Dane," I answer. I flop onto my bed and kick off my shoes all in one motion.

"Hey. Can I see you again?"

I sigh. "I'm sorry. I just don't think it's a good idea. I don't want to send you the wrong message."

"What's the wrong message?"

I pause before I answer. Will my sentiments here change if things go south with Ben at the end of this thing? *Is* there an end to this thing? That's sort of the risk I'm taking here.

It's not fair to Dane to let him fall into the back-up zone, but I'm not exactly sure that's what I'm doing. I'll always hold a special place for him in my heart. He's the one who got me through one of the hardest years of my life.

He held my hand. He made me laugh. He wiped my tears. He listened as I shared my memories.

But Ben incites different feelings in me. Dane feels like a part of my past. Is Ben my future? He is for the next five months. Beyond that…it's a tossup.

"The wrong message is that there's a chance for us to get back together," I finally say.

"So there's not a single chance at all? Even when things end with Olson?"

"Why are you so sure things will end with Ben?" I ask.

"Because he's Ben Olson," he says. "His reputation precedes him, Kay."

"You don't know him."

"No, I don't. You're right. But I know *you*, and I know the things that are important to you. I know you ended our relationship because you wanted things I didn't want. Does Olson want those things?"

No. He doesn't. But I'm not about to admit that to Dane. "That's between Ben and me."

"Fair enough," he concedes. "Can we just talk in person?"

"Why? What possible good will it do?"

He clears his throat. "I have some things I want to say to you."

I blow out a breath. I feel like this meeting needs to be private, but I'm not about to invite him over to Jack's house. I really need a place of my own, but instead of getting that, I'm about to move in with Ben.

"Fine," I finally say. "I'll come to your hotel. Give me a half hour."

It's as I'm in the car on the way there that I realize going to his hotel is absolutely sending the wrong message, but it's too late to back out now.

CHAPTER 22

Kaylee

I valet my car at the Silverton and hop onto an empty elevator car. I brace myself for whatever it is he wants to talk about as the elevator skids to a halt on the eleventh floor. I blow out a breath as the doors open, and I double check my text message for his room number.

When I look up, I see Dane waiting for me in the hallway. He moves in toward me and wraps his arms around me in a hug. It's a little over the line to be considered friendly, but it's not completely out of place given our history.

He grabs my hand. "Come on," he says. I pull my hand out of his grasp and follow him, clutching my purse tightly in both hands just so I have the excuse not to hold his hand—not that I should need one.

He leads me to his room, and he fumbles with his keycard a second before he gets the door to unlock. He holds the door open to allow me to step in first, forcing me to brush past his torso on my way in. It's a lot of close contact given the fact that I've told him I'm in a relationship with somebody else.

At least he hasn't tried to kiss me.

Yet.

I spot a sitting chair by the window, so I head there. That way I'm not on the bed and not on the couch—I'm not in a place where he can inch his knee over toward mine or get the wrong idea about why I showed up. "What do you want to talk about?" I ask.

He clears his throat. "The other day when I saw you for the first time since we broke up at your school…a lot of feelings were reawakened in me. I told you I wasn't going to give up without a fight, and I won't. You keep telling me it's him, but I see it in your eyes, Kay. You still have feelings for me."

"Of course I do, Dane. I'll always have feelings for you. You got me through a very difficult time in my life, and I will always hold that close to my heart. But that doesn't mean there's a future for us. And even if the feelings were still there, even if I wanted to leave the person I've fallen for to be with you…logistically it doesn't even make sense. You're in Chicago. I'm in Vegas." I shrug.

He nods. "That's why I put in for a transfer to the Vegas office Monday night. I found out this morning I got it."

My eyes widen. "So you're moving to Vegas? Just like that?"

"Yeah." He walks over toward me and kneels in front of me. "I'm moving to Vegas. I want to be with you. I want to give you the future you've always dreamed of. I want us to face whatever hard times life throws at us with you, and I want to share in the joy of the good times with you."

My chest tightens as he says words that sound like vows. I'm terrified he's about to reach into his pocket and pull out a ring. And you know what? A year ago, I would've said yes if he did. It was everything I wanted with him.

But life has a funny way of working out the way it's supposed to.

Thankfully, rather than reaching into his pocket, he reaches for my hands. He pulls them to his lips. "Just don't close the book on us, Kaylee."

I pull my hands back out of his reach, and he straightens then stands.

"The book was already long closed," I say softly. I stand. "I don't know how many times I have to say this, but I am with somebody else now. I have fallen in love with him, and I want a future with him. I'm so sorry that isn't what you want to hear, but I don't think you should move here to Vegas. I don't even know if *I* am staying in Vegas, to be honest."

His brows dip. "Where would you go? Back to Michigan?"

I press my lips together and tilt my head as my eyes soften a little at him. "I don't know. But it's none of your concern, okay? Not anymore. I need to go."

I rush out of the room and don't look back. I practically run toward the elevator, and I take it down, get my car from valet, and peel out of the Silverton before anybody can try to stop me.

And instead of driving on toward Jack's house, I find my car navigating its way toward Ben's place.

When I ring the bell, I hear Buddy's bark. The door opens a moment later, and there stands Jeb. In all the craziness of the last couple weeks, I completely forgot that Ben's dad and my mom are going on a date tomorrow night.

Gross.

"Good evening," he says, opening the door a little wider to invite me in as he pulls on Buddy's collar to calm him down.

"Hi, Mr. Olson. Is Ben around?" I kneel down to Buddy's level and scratch his ears. He immediately calms down for me.

"Call me Jeb," he says. "He's in the shower. Should be down any minute. Come on in."

I follow him in. He settles into the recliner, and I sit on the couch. Buddy sits beside me so I can keep scratching his head. "So, uh, you're going to dinner with my mom tomorrow night, right?" I blurt.

Good one, Kay.

He nods. "I hope you don't take it the wrong way. We're both just looking for friendship."

"You do you," I say, holding up a hand with an awkward smile. *But please don't do my mom.*

I guess everybody deserves a chance at love, but now that Ben and I have admitted our feelings for each other, this feels even weirder.

God, Ben. Where are you? This should teach me never to drop by unannounced, but since I'm moving in here soon, I guess I'll probably get to know Jeb.

He chuckles. "I'm glad I ran into you." He talks pointedly and in short sentences.

"Oh?" I say.

He nods. "You seem to be making Ben happy. I see something changing in my son. Keep doing what you're doing."

I'm curious as to how much he knows. Did Ben tell him we're secretly boning? Does he think we're dating because of the media? Or does he think we're just friends?

"He makes me happy, too." I smile, and Buddy rests his chin on my leg. "And so do you," I say in that silly voice reserved for dogs and babies.

"Dad, you still here?" Ben's voice yells from upstairs.

"Yes," Jeb yells back.

We hear his footsteps coming down the stairs along with his voice. "Hey, what's something I can cook for a chick if I'm trying to show her how I feel but don't want to look like I'm trying too hard?" He appears in the doorway at the end of his question, and his eyes widen as he spots me sitting on his couch casually petting Buddy's ears.

I clear my throat. "You can start by not calling her a *chick*."

Jeb laughs.

"I didn't know you were here, but for the record, I was talking about you." He shrugs, ever maintaining his cool. The guy is unflappable when it comes to embarrassing himself, and it's probably because he's done it enough times all on his own.

"My advice would be Italian," Jeb says.

I nod. "You can never go wrong with Italian. Or shrimp. Or cupcakes."

His brows draw together. "Cupcakes?"

I shrug. "My favorite dessert. Especially with chocolate."

"I feel a new nickname coming on," he murmurs, and I giggle. "To what do I owe the pleasure of your surprise visit?"

"I, uh…had some things I wanted to talk to you about," I say.

Jeb takes that as his cue. He stands. "I'll leave you two alone."

"What about poker?" Ben asks.

How freaking adorable is that? Ben and his dad get together to play poker.

"Come over later, or we can play tomorrow."

"Before or after your date?" Ben teases.

"It's just two friends." Jeb sounds exasperated, and I can't imagine how many times his son has caused his parents exasperation in his lifetime.

"Right," Ben says, drawing out the word. "Now get out of here so I can show Kaylee what friendship really means in the Olson family."

My cheeks burn red as Jeb pats Ben on his back. "What you two do should stay between you two," Jeb says.

"Have a good night, Mr. Olson," I mutter as I stare down at my lap.

"You too," he says, and Ben walks him out. I keep petting Buddy, and Ben appears in front of me a minute later.

He whistles to Buddy, who moves to his side. He puts some dog food in Buddy's bowl before he moves toward me. "What's going on?" he asks. Instead of sitting beside me, he sits on the edge of the coffee table in front of me. He leans forward, elbows on his knees with his hands clasped in front of him as he awaits my statement expectantly.

"I went to see Dane just now and I felt like I should tell you," I blurt.

He tilts his head at me. "Okay," he says cautiously. "Did anything happen?"

I shake my head. "He hugged me when I got off the elevator. He tried to hold my hand. I told him I was with you in no uncertain terms." I clear my throat. "He told me he put in for a transfer to Vegas. I told him not to move here."

Ben's brows arch. "He *what?*"

"He said he's going to fight for me." I shrug.

"The dude's a fucking creep. Tell him to back off."

I nod. "I know it seems that way, but like I've told you, I often felt like I wasn't the priority in my own family. We were together for over a year, and we had conversations where I admitted that I just wanted someone to fight for me for once, to make me feel like I was important enough to matter. I really think that's what he's doing. He's trying to make me feel the things I always told him I wanted to feel."

"Do you?" he asks.

I look down at my hands for a beat before I look up at Ben. I lean forward on my elbows, too, so I'm mirroring him. I snag my bottom lip between my teeth for a beat as I think through my answer. We're inches apart, and his fresh scent attacks my senses. I shake my head a little. "I didn't...not until this whole thing started with you."

His forehead wrinkled with concern smooths as his eyes soften. He leans forward to press a gentle kiss to my lips.

"I don't want to be with him, Ben," I say softly. "I want to be with you."

He reaches forward and pulls me onto his lap like I weigh nothing. He cradles me in his arms and kisses me again. "I want to be with you, too."

Buddy whines, and we both laugh. "Come on over, boy," I say, and he wags his tail before he darts across the room toward us. He uses his muzzle to break the link of Ben's arms around me, and warm laughter fills the room as Ben holds me against him and we both pet the dog.

It's such a sweet and idyllic setting that I wish this warm feeling in my chest could last forever.

But like all good things, this too will come to an end.

CHAPTER 23

Ben

"That asshole," I murmur.

He set her up.

I watch the segment Ellie just texted me on the little screen on my phone for a second time as I reach into the box of S'mores cereal and cram a handful into my mouth.

"Billy Peters snapping at you with the latest in the Ben Olson mystery woman saga. My sources were right. The mystery woman is in fact Kaylee Dalton, younger sister of delicious football star brothers Jack and Luke Dalton. And when I say younger, I mean an entire *decade* younger. We knew the Big O liked 'em young, but she would've been twelve the first time they met." A barf emoji flashes across the screen. That dumbfuck. She's not fucking twelve now. We're not doing anything wrong.

"But I'm getting off track. Have you seen the latest from her Insta?" Photos flash on the screen of Kaylee with each of her brothers and then one of her with me. "They look so cozy and cute, don't they?" The screen flashes back to Billy as he snaps his fingers. "So who is *this*?" New photos flash across the screen. She's wearing the same clothes she was wearing last night when she came over out of the blue, but she's hugging a man that isn't me. She's holding his hand as they walk down a hotel hallway. She's ducking into a hotel room as the man looks at the camera.

And *that* is the one that tells me this she was set up.

Billy continues his narration of events. "I don't have a name yet, but my people are on it. If sister Dalton is so cozy with the Big O, why was she spotted going into another man's hotel room yesterday? Stay tuned for the latest in this developing story." He snaps his fingers and moves onto the next victim in his stupid little celebrity gossip show.

I decide to double down with a picture on my own Instagram. She took one of us last night with Buddy when we were all sitting together, and she texted it to me just before she went back home to Jack's place. It was supposed to be a private memory for the two of us, but now the world can see how goddamn happy we are together.

I don't even need to think about my caption before I post it.

Perfect night in last night with my girl.

Fuck Billy Peters and his stupid gossip. She told me what happened, and her ex clearly set her up. He probably called the fucking paparazzi in some stupid attempt to try to come between us.

The devil works hard, but I work harder.

I FaceTime Ellie. She's sitting at her desk when she picks up. "Hey, Ben," she answers.

"Her ex set us up."

"But she *did* meet him at a hotel, didn't she?" Ellie asks.

"It was innocent. She came by after to tell me what went down."

"She did?" Ellie asks.

Of course she did, but I can't admit the reason why—that we're really together now and she tells me shit like that because we're honest with each other. "Yeah. She just wanted to make sure our deal was protected. She said he put in for a transfer and he's moving to Vegas and wants to fight for her."

Ellie sighs. "Does she want to be with him?"

"Doesn't sound like it. I asked her that too. Told her I didn't want this deal between us to get in the way of what she wants for her future." That much is true…but I conveniently leave out a few other facts.

"Is she okay with continuing on with the charade?" Ellie asks.

I nod.

"Okay, good. She's at school now so I haven't sent this to her yet, but I was thinking after school I could meet her at a bridal shop and maybe call in a few…*photographers* of our own. Is that okay with you?" Ellie asks. She's staring at me through the little screen.

I blow out a breath as I glance away. I don't like this, but it is what it is. "I gave her the green light to drop hints. Do what you need to do."

"But is it okay with you? I mean…I know where you stand on the whole marriage thing, and since this is all just an act, I don't want to push you outside of your comfort zone."

I let out a sarcastic guffaw. "I have yet to find my comfort zone with any of this, Ellie."

She presses her lips together and nods. "I know. But has Calvin called you since your relationship hit the press?"

I shake my head.

"Thought as much," she says. "Listen, you're doing great. We'll set up a photoshoot this weekend. Your place? Something like you two at home."

"Nah." I glance around at the place I call home. It's fine. It's a rental. It's not *home*. "My place isn't really *me*, you know? Jack's place, a hotel, whatever. But not here."

A lightbulb seems to click on over her head. "Oh, what about when we're in Montana? We could do some shoots there. Is that more *you*?"

I nod. "It's about as *me* as it gets, but not at my house. That's private."

"Got it. On your property?"

I shrug. "That's fine." Better than inviting every stranger with a curious mind into my home.

"I'll schedule something for the month we're there. But in the meantime, I'll find a place and a photographer who can work on short notice with you two. Hopefully tomorrow so we can get a jump on posting and get freaking Billy Peters to shut up about the two of you."

"How are her sponsorships coming along?" I ask.

"Offers are starting to roll in and she doubled her follows since posting that selfie of the two of you last night."

My brows rise. "Where's she at now?"

"Close to twenty thousand. Thirty is considered an official Instagram celebrity according to the Advertising Standards Authority, so once she clears that threshold, we have more regulations to adhere to. I've got a sponsor drawing up a quick contract but I'm waiting to hit thirty so we can hold out for bigger offers. And I have a bunch of interest in you, too. I know you said you wanted a few new ones just for your competition with Kaylee, and I'm working hard to keep you on brand."

"You're good at what you do," I say. "And I appreciate it."

She smiles. "Just doing what I love to do. Now stay out of trouble and I'll be in touch."

I chuckle. "I'll try." I was trying to stay out of trouble last night, which was why I invited my dad over for poker. It's hard to get into trouble when you're hanging with your old man.

But after this set up by her ex...I feel the sudden urge to get into a *little* trouble—only not the kind of trouble I used to get into.

Instead of the party boy image that I've cultivated over the years, if I act on the feelings inside of me, I'll get into trouble for different reasons.

She came to me upset last night because of what her ex said to her. She doesn't want to be with him. She wants to be with me.

And after she explained what happened and I held her in my arms and we didn't even get naked, I realized that all this goes a lot deeper than I first thought.

I'm not a violent man, but I'll do whatever it takes to protect Kaylee.

CHAPTER 24

Kaylee

I'm fuming with anger. It's a Friday afternoon and the last kid just left my room after asking me who the man in the hotel was. It took me all of four seconds to find the latest Billy Peters video with images of me and Dane.

I don't even question *why* he did it. He said he's going to fight for me, and obviously this is his way. He's trying to break Ben and me up by planting certain seeds, but he's going to have to try a lot harder than that to come between us.

He has no idea I went straight to Ben's place after I saw him at his hotel. He has no idea that I felt pulled to confess to my *boyfriend* that another man issued a wager to fight for my heart.

It was like I didn't even have a choice. My car just navigated itself to his house so I could fill him in, and as he held me in his arms and Buddy nuzzled my hand, a new bond formed between us.

It was like I physically felt that initial layer of sexual tension between us morph into something raw and real. The sexual tension is still there—there's no denying that—but now it's paired with *feelings*. Real feelings that seem to dig their way deeper and deeper every day.

It's my last week of school. Less than one week until summer. Less than one week until the rest of my life can begin.

And the more time I spend around the Big O, the more time I want that to include him.

So he's old and he listens to Nickelback. Nobody's perfect.

A text from Ellie comes through as I'm holding my phone in my hand after having just finished the video.

Ellie: *I waited until school was over to send you the latest.*

There's a link to the video I just watched attached.

Me: *I just saw it. A student asked me who the man at the hotel was. [eyeroll emoji]*

Ellie: *I'm on damage control. Can you meet Kate and me at Happily Ever After Bridal Boutique in an hour? I *might* have called in a few photographer friends of my own. [purple devil emoji]*

She attaches an address to the text. I click it, and it's only fifteen minutes from school.

Me: *I'll be there. [bride emoji]*

I wrap up what I'm working on, run copies for next week which include final exams, and bring another box of binders to Ashley's room. And then I navigate toward the address Ellie sent me.

When I arrive, I spot her car in the parking lot. I pull in next to her, and she smiles and waves frantically at me. I giggle, and I wave back to both her and Kate, who sits in the passenger seat.

The three of us get out of our cars at the same time and hug in the parking lot, taking our time to ensure the logo of the store is centered in the background of where we stand. Dane thought he could win this round, but he's playing alone. I've got a team on my side.

We stand in the parking lot and make small talk for a few minutes to give the photographers Ellie tipped off plenty of time to get our photos, and then we head inside.

And it's a freaking dreamland.

Wedding gowns in every shape, style, and size line rack after rack after rack. The side wall is entirely mirrored, so it looks like the dresses go on forever and ever. In the center of the mirrored wall is a circular platform with luxurious, pale pink couches pointed at it.

"Welcome in," a woman greets us, and she nods toward the couches. "I'm Delinda and I'll be taking care of you today. Come have a seat."

We head toward the couches, and there's a table set up in front of them with all sorts of magazines and binders on it. Delinda offers us champagne, which both Kate and Ellie decline since they have to get back to work after this little outing.

I decline, too, since I have to drive home.

It's not like this is a real dress shopping appointment. I'd want my mom there for that, anyway.

"What styles do you like?" Delinda asks me.

I stare at her blankly.

"This is just our first stop," Ellie explains, swooping in to save the day. "We haven't really done a lot of research yet, so I think Kaylee was hoping you'd be able to guide her a little."

"Of course." She grabs a binder. "Let's look at style first. Are you thinking more of a ball gown, an A-line, a mermaid, a sheath, or something else?" She points to images of each style as she talks, and I point to the ball gown.

"Perfect. Next is the neckline. Strapless, V-neck, scoop, sweetheart, halter?" She points to each one again, and I point to the V-neck.

"Train or no train?" she asks.

I shrug. "Maybe a little one?"

She nods. "Materials?"

"Any."

"Sparkles?" she asks.

"Of course." I say it like the answer is obvious, and both Kate and Ellie giggle.

"Let me pull you a few samples." She eyes me as if she's sizing me up, and then she takes off. Ellie picks up a magazine to flip through it, and Kate does the same while I blow out a breath.

I've never tried on wedding gowns before. I've never been shopping for them—not even for a friend or relative. Ellie and Luke's wedding was a secret surprise, and Jack and Kate also got married for the first time in secret. Ellie and Luke had a fun reception on their one-year anniversary last summer, and Kate and Jack are planning a celebration this summer, too, but the actual dress shopping has never been on my radar.

Even though I was having fun with Dane back when we were together and before I knew we wanted different things out of life, of course I imagined him proposing to me someday. What girl doesn't dream of that when they find someone they've started to fall for?

But breaking up with him made me realize that I'm still young and that there doesn't need to be some big rush to get down the aisle. Still, though, given that I want a whole litter of kids—four or five, at least—I'm also not getting any younger. I always dreamed of being a young mom. Some people are immature for their ages, and others are the opposite…and maybe that's what makes Ben my perfect match.

Except he doesn't want four or five kids. He doesn't even want *one*, and the thought of even a *pretend* marriage had him freaking terrified.

So even though every other signal seems to be telling me we're perfect for each other, it's the big ones telling me we're not.

Delinda returns with a rack a moment later. Five or six hangers are on it, all hidden behind a black garment bag at the front of the rack. "Here's what I found that looks to be around your size. Let me know if you see any you'd like to try on." She pulls the first one out, and my jaw drops.

It's gorgeous. It's dreamy and elegant, romantic with its lace bodice and lace straps with a sparkly design on the torso that layers down along with the lace design. It's a tiered design that will give the dress volume while still maintaining a contemporary style.

I love it.

I don't even need to try it on. I don't need to see the other ones.

This is *the* dress.

Except…I'm not getting married.

And for some reason, a dart of sadness pings my chest at the thought.

"Oh, that's beautiful," Kate murmurs. "You better grab it before I do."

I laugh off that sad feeling. "It's very pretty," I say, downplaying my real feelings. "Can we see the others?"

She shows them off. They're all beautiful, too, but they're not the showstopping stunner that first one was.

"Want to take them into the fitting room?" Delinda asks, and I nod.

I don't try *the one* on first…as silly as it sounds, I know there are photographers just outside the window, and I know they'll be snapping photos through the window of every dress I try on.

I'm not hugely superstitious, but I don't want them getting my photo in that one. I don't want it splashed on the tabloids.

The groom isn't supposed to see the dress before the big day, after all. Maybe it's silly, but it's a chance I just don't want to take. Not when the odds are already stacked up against us.

CHAPTER 25

Ben

I canceled my plans with my buddies.

Anyone who knows me knows I don't do that, and *that* is what the real shocker here is.

I keep telling myself it's to maintain our façade, but let's be honest. There are two reasons I care about the game we're playing with the media. The first is because competition is one of my top strengths. I want to win, which is part of what makes me the football player I am.

But that's not why I canceled my plans. Hell, I could've invited Kaylee along…but instead, I decided to ask her on our second public date.

The second reason, therefore, is because I'm feeling things for Kaylee that are unfamiliar. I want to see her again. I want to *be with* her again. I want her to spend the night again. I want to wake up with her in my bed.

I really want to fuck her in my shower. We haven't done that yet, and my shower is fucking badass. Two shower heads plus one of those handheld shower heads (perfect for clitoral stimulation, or so I'm told).

I haven't even asked her yet, and this isn't for an official event, but a friend of mine opened a restaurant on the Strip and I told him I'd stop by at some point. It's great press for him, and it's good food for me and my date.

I shoot over a text on Friday afternoon.

Me: *Are you free for dinner out tonight? We can give them something to talk about.*

Her reply isn't immediate, but Ellie mentioned something about wedding dresses. The initial thought of that scared the ever living fuck out of me, but I'm starting to get used to the idea.

Which also scares the ever living fuck out of me.

Kaylee: *Only if we can get into some trouble.*

Yeah…I definitely think I can provide trouble.

Me: *As you know, that's my real first name.*

Kaylee: *[laughing emoji] Well aware of that fact, T.*

I laugh.

Me: *Come over so we can get into a little trouble before we go. Bring an overnight bag.*

Kaylee: *I'm currently wrapped in organza and tulle also to give them something to talk about, but I'll swing home, change, and then be on my way. Six-ish?*

Me: *I have no idea what the fuck tulle is but yeah, six works.*

I Google tulle.

Jesus. I am so fucked.

* * *

I texted Ellie my plans for the night with the understanding she'd tip off the paparazzi to ensure our photos end up in the press tomorrow. It's a great way to get some attention on my pal's restaurant while feeding into the frenzy surrounding my relationship with Kaylee…or at least what we want people to think.

The actual truth is even more complicated than it seems.

My bell rings a little after six, and before I open it, I peek out the peephole. I spot my girl standing on my porch in a glorious little sexy red dress. The same car that's been parked across the street all day is still there, and so I toss the door open and pull Kaylee into my arms to give them a bit of a show.

My mouth crashes down to hers, and I pull her inside with our lips connected before I slam the door behind her.

And even when it's closed, I don't let go. Instead, I take it deeper. More urgent. More intense. I back her into the door and shove my hips against her as my body's response to her familiar scent takes hold. Her hands reach under my shirt and claw at my back, and *fuck* does it feel good to have her back in my arms.

My chest tightens at the thought.

She moves her arms to link them around my neck then jumps and wraps her legs around my waist. "I'm not wearing panties," she murmurs.

A low growl rumbles up out of my chest on its own accord, and she lets out a soft moan when I thrust my hips against hers.

The good kind of sexual tensions swirls around us, and this time, it's just for the two of us.

I reach under to plunge a finger into her, and I get a loud moan as she drenches my hand. I thrust in and out of her as I kiss her, adding a second finger which is rewarded with another moan as her tongue continues to batter mine.

I pull my fingers out and manage to unbutton my pants. I pull my cock out and shove it into her without warning, and it's like I'm fucking home again.

She cries out with approval as I start to move, and she's so slick and wet and tight that I know I'm not going to last long. The pure feeling of utter perfection with nothing separating the two of us just isn't meant to last forever. If it did, we'd have nothing to look forward to.

I fuck her up against my front door, driving into her with my hands under her ass to bounce her up and down on my cock. She breaks from our kiss as her cries get louder and faster as I drive her toward her climax. She leans her head back, thumping it gently against the front door, and I think I black out from pleasure for a second before that familiar heat pushes my balls up. I thumb at her clit and I explode into her as my release hits me.

I grunt my way through it as pulse after pulse of pleasure bursts through my body, and I hit her clit just right as it pushes her into her orgasm while I'm riding the wave of mine. Her pussy clenches over me, milking every last drop of come from my cock.

My mouth falls to hers again, and we kiss slowly and intimately while I'm still inside her.

With her...I think this is my favorite part of sex. When I start to come back down to Earth, my body rubbery and sated, and we kiss with all this tenderness. It's like a thank you for the incredible sex while showing her how deep my feelings are starting to become—something I need since I can't seem to find the words to tell her.

I'm not sure the words exist. At least not in my vocabulary.

"I know we said three more weeks until you move in, but I don't want to wait that long," I say against her mouth.

"Me either," she murmurs, and I kiss her a little longer before I slip out and set her down on her feet. She leans against the front door while she smooths her dress back down.

"This weekend," I say, leaning in for one more kiss as I tuck my dick back into my pants. "You're here all the time anyway and this way you wouldn't have to pack an overnight bag."

This isn't for the media. This isn't for show. This is for us.

She nods. "Let's do it."

We take a brief walk through my house and talk about where we can put her stuff. To keep up the ruse we're faking for her family, she'll take the guest room as "her" bedroom even though she'll stay with me.

She freshens up while I change my clothes and throw some food in Buddy's bowl, and then we head out to dinner.

The car that's been parked across the street all day follows us. It's not a huge surprise, though it is a huge invasion of our privacy. It comes with the territory.

I make conversation on the way over. "You know what tonight is?"

She glances at me. "What?"

"Your mom and my dad's first date."

She wrinkles her nose, and I laugh.

"It's not a date. My mom assured me over and over and over once more."

"My dad said your mom seemed pretty interested." I wiggle my eyebrows.

"Oh God." She presses her hand to her forehead in a facepalm. "I don't want to know about it. Does your dad know about us?"

"Yeah."

"The *whole* truth?" she presses.

"Yeah." I reach over and lay a palm on her thigh, and she rests her hand on top of mine. "I mean, not the fact that I've now fucked you up against my front door more than once, but he knows I have real feelings for you. And he knows we're hiding those feelings from the people closest to us."

I pull in front of the hotel where the restaurant is located, effectively ending our conversation as I valet the Scout. I help her out of the passenger door while I toss my keys to valet with some joke about keeping my vehicle safe, and when we turn around, we're faced with flashbulbs. Thanks, Ellie.

I link my hand with hers and lead her inside the hotel and toward the restaurant. My buddy knows I'm coming tonight, and he's waiting near the hostess stand when we arrive.

"Mr. Olson," Michael Cordell says with a very businesslike nod.

"Fuck off, Cordell," I say, and he laughs.

"I'm Mike Cordell, the owner of this joint," he says to Kaylee.

"Kaylee Dalton," she says with a smile as she shakes his hand.

"Right this way." We follow him through the restaurant to a table in the center of the action where he wants me to be seen dining in his establishment. To my disappointment, there's no way I'll be able to do any of the things I want to do to my date under the table with our seat location where it is.

"Can I start you with a beverage?" he asks.

It's a fancy place, but I'm still a beer guy. "What's on tap?" I ask. He names a bunch of beers, and I say, "Surprise me." I glance at Kaylee with raised brows.

"Something red and not too dry," she says, and Mike nods.

"You got it. Enjoy your meals, and really, Ben, thanks for coming. It means a lot."

I nod and offer a smile, and a waiter comes up behind the boss. Mike saunters off while our waiter offers his suggestions for our meals, and we both order without even looking at a menu.

"So how do you know the owner?" Kaylee asks.

"Oh, we met seven or eight years ago. He owned a nightclub I frequented when I was in town. He wanted to expand into restaurants, and now he owns a handful of clubs and this is his second restaurant here in Vegas."

Another dude drops our drinks by, and she holds up her glass of red while she waits expectantly for me to say something.

I hold up my glass, too. "To proving them wrong."

She giggles and nods. "Amen." We clink glasses and each take a sip, and Mike sent me over some lighter beer that's a little overly crafty for my taste but will do the job. I'm pretty simple, my preference leading toward Budweiser, but I'll drink pretty much anything.

"How's the wine?" I ask.

"Not too dry, a little sweet. Just about perfect." She takes another sip and moves to set it down.

"Sounds like your pussy," I murmur, and she coughs a little on her last sip. I let out a chuckle. I clear my throat. "How was your shopping trip today?" I ask a little louder for the benefit of anyone listening…and there's always somebody listening.

She stiffens a little, and part of me wonders what that's all about. Is she as freaked out by the wedding shit as I am? Somehow I doubt it. Knowing what I know about her, she probably loved every second. "It was fun. Kate and Ellie are the best."

"Did you find a dress?"

Her eyes twinkle as they connect with mine. "Guess you'll have to wait and see."

I chuckle. "What are your plans for next weekend?"

She shrugs. "School's out Friday, I'll be done with the career I can't stand, and my birthday is Saturday. I don't have plans yet, but clearly something epic is on my agenda."

"It's your birthday?" I ask, lowering my voice a little since as her *boyfriend* I should know this, and she nods. "Then we'll figure out something epic. Leave it to me."

She narrows her eyes at me. "Why does that terrify me a little?"

159

I shrug innocently, but she's probably right to be a little scared.

CHAPTER 26

Kaylee

I stayed the night nestled in Ben's warm arms, and in the morning, he treats me to his normal morning routine…which happens to be cereal and cartoons.

He pulls up some old episode of *Looney Tunes* on YouTube.

"Cartoons?" I ask.

He shrugs. "They remind me of a simpler time, and Daffy is the shit."

I laugh. "I'm more of a *Tom and Jerry* girl myself."

"Tom and Jerry?" he asks. "But they're enemies. You strike me more as a girl who would enjoy a happy ending."

"I am. Did you know the cat and the mouse are actually best friends?"

His brows knit together. "In what alternate universe is that true?"

"Uh, this one," I say. "Tom was *pretending* to hate Jerry so his owner wouldn't kill the mouse himself."

He tilts his head as he contemplates that for a beat. "I feel like my entire childhood was a lie."

I giggle as we move into the kitchen to grab breakfast, and he pulls a blue box of cereal out of the pantry.

"This is what I eat when I don't prepare fresh croissants or something greasy to cure a hangover. And incidentally, I also eat this for a nighttime snack fairly often, sometimes with milk and sometimes without. And after lunch." He shrugs. "Okay, fine, I go through a box a day." He holds up the box.

"S'mores?" I read.

He nods. "Only the best cereal on this planet." He pours a bowl for me, and I spot cocoa puffs, golden grahams, and marshmallows. I nab a marshmallow since those little dehydrated, crunchy marshmallows are the best part of any cereal that contains them.

He pours a bowl for himself, too, and I steal a marshmallow out of his bowl. "What the fuck are you doing?" he demands, and I giggle at his tone.

"Milk?" he asks.

I shake my head and start picking at the cereal, grabbing the cocoa puffs first as he watches me.

"What are you doing?"

My brows dip at his question. "What? I'm eating it from worst to best. Cocoa puffs first, then the golden grahams, and the marshmallows last."

"The marshmallows are *not* the best part," he counters.

My brows knit together a little angrily. "If you don't think so, then hand yours over, Olson."

He laughs. "No way! It's the mixture of all the flavors coming together that does it for me." He grabs a handful directly from the box and shoves it in his mouth.

"What kind of animal eats cereal like that?" I ask.

"The kind you like to fuck," he counters.

I laugh and we settle in to watch some cartoons as we enjoy our cereal. I have to admit…it's a stress-free, fun way to start the day.

He follows me to Jack's house for their weekly workout. My plan is to pack up the remaining items I unpacked when I lost the apartment, and Ben said we can probably fit most of my belongings into his truck.

It's sort of sad when I think of it that way.

I'm an adult now. I'm ready to start my life, to get a place of my own, to figure out my own path…and instead, I'm embarking on another temporary housing situation. I don't want it to be temporary, and the more time I spend with Ben both in public and in private, the more I wish there wasn't an end looming ahead of us.

Ben follows me as I unlock the front door and walk through the house. Kate is on the floor in the family room playing with JJ while Jack drinks some protein shake in the kitchen.

"Good morning," she says on our way by. "Have you heard from your mom yet?"

I wrinkle my nose. "Not yet."

"Didn't want to wake her up if she's still over at my dad's place," Ben says dryly.

Kate laughs. "I can't wait to hear how it went. And have you two seen the latest?"

I narrow my eyes at her. "What latest?"

She sighs, pulls something up on her phone, and screen mirrors it to the television. We all watch as that dumbass gossip vlogger appears on the screen.

"The newest *it* couple is at it again, folks." Billy Peters snaps his fingers. "First Little Sister Dalton was spotted heading into a bridal shop in Vegas." The face screaming in fear emoji appears on the screen only to fade to another photo. It's fuzzy and clearly taken through a window, but it's me in a dress.

Not *the* dress, but a dress all the same.

Ben shifts uncomfortably, and I really want to study him to try to decode what he's thinking but my brother is moving in closer to us and Kate's right there…so I keep my eyes on the screen.

"Dress shopping already?" Billy says. "This screams set-up to me. What about you? Cast your vote in my Instagram stories."

He snaps his fingers again and a photo of Ben and me with our heads bent close together at the restaurant appears on the screen. I'm looking up at him with something close to adoration in my fairy freshly fucked state, and he's gazing down at me with a bit of a smirk on his face. Clearly there's something between us from the look of the photo, and I'm a little uncomfortable for a second that my brother is standing mere feet away watching this. "They were spotted last night at Cordell's, the hottest new restaurant on the Vegas Strip." Billy snaps again and a flopping fish appears on the screen before it fades away to Billy's face. "I smell something fishy. We've never seen them out before last weekend and now they're hitting the town, dining in fancy new restaurants, wedding dress shopping, and looking all in love? Sources are screaming that it's all a show, and I'm going to get to the bottom of it."

He snaps his fingers and moves onto the next celebrity story.

Jeez.

Who cares if we're faking it? How does it affect Billy's life *really*?

Billy is the one putting our relationship under a microscope—our *perceived* relationship, anyway—while something between really is blossoming in private. It's a very strange dynamic.

Kate turns off the video, and I roll my eyes. "I swear to God I don't know anybody who cares *this much* about a celebrity's life."

"Aww, you think I'm a celebrity?" Ben asks.

"I was talking about myself, you know, Little Sister Dalton." I roll my eyes at the description Billy labeled me with in that stupid video that's probably already going viral. It's the label I'm trying hardest to escape, and it seems to keep popping up, keeping a thumb on me to ground me in reality.

It makes me feel like I will never outgrow that label, and I hate it.

This is all just a part of why I don't date football players…and yet I'm doing it. Publicly. And falling for him.

"Yeah, little sister to the famous Dalton brothers who's now a celebrity herself," Kate says. She holds up her phone, and her Instagram app is open.

My brows dip. "I did it?"

She nods and looks at the screen. "Thirty-three thousand, two hundred four."

My eyes widen. "Holy shit. People actually care about my content?"

"Congratulations," Kate says with a nod. "You're officially Insta-famous!"

"Congratulations," Ben echoes. He puts up his hand for a high-five, and I slap it with a giggle.

My phone buzzes in my pocket with a notification I ignore.

"So my Insta-famous girlfriend and I decided to move up our move-in date to shut up the rumors," Ben blurts.

Jack nods as he steps into place beside Ben. "Probably a good idea if you're sticking to the plan. Who knows what that asshole has up his sleeve next?" He gestures toward the television with his protein shake. He looks at me. "When are you moving?"

Ben and I exchange a glance. "Today," we say at the same time.

Jack and Kate exchange a glance this time. "Holy shit, Kia. That means as soon as *tonight* we're going to have this place to ourselves."

Kate laughs as Jack glances around the house.

"The couch, the kitchen table, the counters…" Jack says, and he keeps looking around. "The floor, the family room table, the pool…"

My nose wrinkles in a little bit of disgust. I know what he's doing.

"Hmm…" He pretends to think. "So many options when it's just the two of us once JJ is asleep. I'll go with all of the above. Definitely. But where to do it first? Sex on the floor is never what it's cracked up to be, you know? I'm thinking something a little more comfortable. The couch?"

Kate shakes her head. "Kitchen counter for the win."

"You guys are disgusting," I say, and they both laugh.

But honestly, I can't blame them considering I've already taken stock at Ben's house of all the places we'll be getting busy.

My phone starts to ring, and I glance at my watch to find it's Dane calling. I ignore it.

Fuck him.

He set me up, and he deserves zero more of my time and attention.

He leaves tomorrow to go back to Chicago, and I sincerely hope he took my advice to heart that he shouldn't move here.

At this point, I just feel betrayed. Even if I really *was* faking with Ben, Dane certainly isn't doing himself any favors to try to actually win me back.

He tries again, and I ignore it again. Maybe it's passive aggressive since he has to know I'm ignoring by sending him to voicemail after a couple rings, but I don't care.

"I'll help get boxes down to the Scout once we're done in the weight room," Ben says to me. "Should be done in a couple hours."

I nod. "Okay. I'll get everything packed up." I step toward him to give him a kiss, and I'm inches from actually doing it when it dawns on me that Jack and Kate are in the room. My eyes widen as I slowly move past him and play it off like I was being funny since we're faking it.

It just felt so natural to kiss my boyfriend as we part for the next couple hours…but in front of these people, he's not my boyfriend.

A big part of me wishes I could be honest about it, but every time I really consider telling them the truth about us, a little voice in the back of my head reminds me how whatever happens between Ben and me could have ripple effects through our entire dynamic. After we all got so close when we lost our dad, I'm just not in a place where I'm ready to mess with what we have now.

And that way, if things go south at the expiration of our deal, or even before that…I won't have to deal with the sympathetic smiles and the sad looks of pity.

This way, I can live in the moment and enjoy what we have even though I'm terrified the end isn't too far off.

CHAPTER 27

Ben

I've known Jack Dalton a long time.

Technically I've known his sister almost as long—just shy by a couple weeks.

Jack and I are close friends.

We lost touch somewhere in the middle of our friendship, but he's the kind of guy who will do *anything* for the people who are important to him. As a teammate, he counts me on that list. But we've transcended the teammate bond to form a different sort of bond.

When we were younger, we'd frequent strip clubs, smoke cigars, chug beer, and make stupid bets. When we got a little older, we'd frequent strip clubs, smoke cigars, chug beer—for me, anyway. He graduated to gin—and make stupid bets.

We played on the same team and then we played for different teams, but when we ended up on the Aces together, it was like no time had passed at all. We went out to a club the night we realized we'd both been traded to the same team. We had a hell of a lot of fun. And then he met Kate the next day, and while our friendship still existed, it changed to something else.

He didn't want to go to the strip clubs with me anymore.

He didn't want to smoke cigars anymore.

He still drank gin, though, and we still had a hell of a good time making stupid bets.

And that's where I land this morning. We're standing in the pool house he converted into his personal workout shed, and I look over at the set of treadmills in front of the mirrored wall.

"Who are the scratches from?" he asks, nodding toward my arm.

"Your sister," I say. It's sort of fun to poke the bear, if I'm being honest, but he obviously thinks I'm just kidding.

"Fuck off, man," he says.

I quickly change the subject. "A hundred bucks says I can run a mile faster than you." I stretch out my calves. I've had a recurring cramp in my calf during workouts this off-season, and Tony tried to explain to me that it's because I drink beer. He said I'm depleting my sodium levels and taking electrolytes from my body without replacing them.

I think he's full of shit and it's just something that comes with age.

Jack laughs as he glances at the treadmill. "You think you're faster than me? You've got twenty-five pounds on me, man."

We're both lean and muscular, and we're close to the same height, but he's right. Our weight is just distributed differently and that couple centimeters I have on him must be where all my weight is.

"You don't think you can beat me?"

He laughs. "Make it a grand and you're on."

I nod, and we each get on a treadmill and start it up. He turns up the music—not Nickelback, to my dismay, but some classic rock—and I warm up by jogging a few paces first while he does the same. "Ready?" I ask.

He nods, and we each click the buttons on the treadmill to program it for one mile. "Set," he says.

"Go!" we both say at the same time, and I crank up the speed on mine as I lower the incline so I'm running on a flat surface. He tilts his to a slight decline so he's running downhill, but I'm focusing less on him and more on my own speed. I'm pacing myself so I can sprint at the end.

It's as I pass the three-quarter-mile mark that my calf starts cramping up.

"Fuck!" I yell, but I run through the pain just like I would if I was in a game.

Jack's concentration doesn't break, and his treadmill slows to a walk before mine does. "Four minutes, thirty-nine seconds," he yells proudly over the music.

"Fuck," I mutter as I glance at my clock that's flashing twelve seconds more than his time. I try to walk off the cramp, but it's not happening.

He turns the music way down. "The calf again?" he asks, and I nod.

He heads over toward a cabinet where he keeps all sorts of vitamins and supplements, and he tosses me a bottle of salt tablets. Then he opens his refrigerator and tosses me a Gatorade.

"Stop drinking beer, dude," he says.

I laugh through the pain paired with the fact that I just lost a thousand dollars. "You sound like Tony."

"Stop thinking it's because you're old. I'm a year older than you and my legs don't cramp like that."

"Because you're fucking perfect," I mutter as I lie on the ground and attempt to stretch it out.

He comes over to help me out the way the trainers do, bracing my leg and moving it backward. "Definitely not perfect," he mutters. "But smarter than you."

I shrug. He's probably right about that.

"Listen, while we're here having this…intimate moment," he begins, and I chuckle through the pain. "What's going on with you and my sister?"

"We're faking a relationship for the benefit of the media so they will lay off my party boy image and I can get Calvin to crawl out of my ass."

"Well that's some imagery," he says. "But not exactly what I was asking."

I shake him off my leg and sit up. "Thanks," I mutter, nodding toward my calf.

"Any better?"

"No. But I'll live." I stretch it back and forth a few times. Fuck do these cramps hurt. I have to figure out how to make this stop before the season starts. More Gatorade might be the key, but less beer is not.

"I know you're faking, but she's moving in with you, and I just wanted to take this opportunity to remind you that she's my little sister and you better keep your hands off her."

"Or what?" I challenge. I realize I'm riding a fine line here, but part of me wants to be honest with him while the other part of me knows I can't.

He doesn't laugh it off the way I expect him to. "Without our dad here, I feel like I need to protect her. And you, too. I don't want anything to fuck up our dynamic on the field, and I don't want to worry about my sister."

"You have nothing to worry about, Jack," I say, finally getting serious with him. And it's the truth. She knows what she's getting into, and the two of us have the potential to hurt each other fiercely. Unfortunately, he can't protect her from whatever's between the two of us. It all feels inevitable, like there's some energy at play we're powerless to stop.

Regardless, though, it's between her and me. Jack doesn't factor into that equation, and neither does his relationship with either of us.

"I have a question for you, though," I say.

His brows knit together.

I stand up to walk off the cramp, but instead it looks like I'm pacing. And I am. I'm nervous to ask this question, but like a man might ask his girlfriend's father…I feel like I need to address this to the person who has put himself into that role. "I know at first you were against this fake relationship idea, but Ellie is putting pressure on me to make it look like we're moving toward the aisle. It's part of why Kaylee's moving in this weekend instead of in a couple weeks. What would you say about the two of us actually getting engaged?"

He blows out a breath. "Jesus. This is Ellie's default, isn't it?"

I press my lips together and nod. "She said it worked for her and Luke. It got the press and Calvin off his back, and that's really all I'm looking to do. Plus raise a bunch of money for charity."

"Charity? The chick at Honeys?" he asks, naming a stripper we used to watch dance across the stage together.

I laugh. "No. I'm thinking more along the lines of a foundation."

He raises his brows, clearly impressed. "And you think getting engaged will help with that?"

"It's an untapped market for a guy like me. I get to capitalize on shit like cigars and tuxedoes and honeymoons and jewelers. We put a new spin on my old endorsements. I can still have the party image with the whiskeys and the beers and of course athletic supplements and gear. And she gets to capitalize on dresses and stylists and hair shit. It's win-win except for the whole, you know, *I don't want to fucking get married* thing."

"Then why would you even consider it?" he asks.

I rub my fingers against my thumb to indicate money. "I finally figured out what I want to do when I retire."

"We do not speak of the *R* word in this shed," Jack says, and he isn't joking.

"The calf cramp is a daily reminder that I'm not getting any younger, man. I've flailed my way through a successful career, but I can't flail my way through what comes next." Shit, that sounds familiar…like someone important said that to me not so long ago.

"But you're not a planner. I've known you a long time, and shit just falls into your lap as if by magic."

He's right. Traditionally, that's how my life has gone. But with Kaylee in it, I want to start looking at the future. I want to look at what comes next. I might even want to lay some plans.

And I want to figure out whether I'm capable of moving forward once this contract between us comes to an end.

CHAPTER 28

Kaylee

I chat with Kate a while before I head upstairs to pack once the boys started their workout, and as excited as I am to move in with Ben, a little part of me is going to miss living at Jack and Kate's house.

Kate has become one of my closest friends. When Jack started high school, which is where football really became his life, I was three. When he went off to college, I was seven. When he was drafted onto the Chargers, I was eleven.

I was never really allowed the chance to get to know him the way I always wanted to, and he's more closed up than Luke, which made it even harder. Luke and I have always been close because even though he was older and busier, he still made the effort to keep the connection open between us. Jack never did that. He hardly ever visited, and when he did, it was always a quick trip so he could return to his life.

But seeing him with his son and with Kate has shown me a whole new side to him. Since we lost our dad, I've seen a big change in him. Maybe it's because he's the oldest son and he feels like he needs to take the role of protector over our family, but whatever the case, I'm glad I've had the last few months to get to know him better.

He's one of the greatest quarterbacks to ever play the game, and he's my brother. How freaking cool is that?

Some of my clothes are still packed from when I almost did this a couple weeks ago, so it doesn't take long to pull what's left out of my drawers and fold them into the suitcases. I tuck the stuffed bear from the hockey game into one of the suitcases before I zip it up and stand it near the door. I grab the hangers in my closet and stack them over the top of the suitcase, and then I head into my bathroom to work on my toiletries.

I knew my living situation was temporary, so I really only unpacked and moved in the essentials. And now I'm moving into another temporary situation.

It just feels more and more like I'm putting my own life on hold.

I've got a temporary boyfriend, a temporary house, and a temporary job. I turn twenty-three in one week, and I have no idea where I want my life to go after September when this is all over.

I'm just about done when I pull out my phone, and I see Dane left a voicemail when he called earlier. It's been nearly two hours since he called, and I finally listen to it.

"I head back home tomorrow. I'm hoping to see you again before I leave, but since you're not answering, I guess I'll have to find some other way to get your attention."

That's it. That's the whole message.

I'm not sure what sort of chaos I unleashed by not answering, but I have an ominous feeling I'll find out soon.

Ben appears freshly showered in my doorway a little while later and he starts carrying boxes down to his car. Jack shows up behind him and carries down the heavy suitcases, and Kate and I drag down the clothes on hangers.

Once everything is packed into the Scout, I turn and look back at Jack and Kate's place. "I'll miss living with you guys. Thanks for letting me crash here as long as you did."

"You're always welcome here," Kate says, pulling me into a hug.

Jack hugs me next in a tight squeeze. "Of course. Come by any time. Just ring the bell first, okay?"

I giggle and I wipe away a tear at the same time as emotions plow into me. I blow out a breath as I click my seatbelt into place.

Ben waits until we've pulled out of the driveway and we're out of their view, and then he reaches over to squeeze my thigh. "You okay?"

I nod and stare out the window a beat. "Yeah. I just haven't gotten to spend that kind of time with my brother since before he started high school. I was probably five or six. It's been great getting to know who he is today."

"He's a good guy," Ben says.

I nod. "The best."

"He warned me off you, you know."

I giggle. "Of course he did. What did you tell him?"

"I told him he has nothing to worry about."

"I'm sorry you had to lie to him," I say softly. "I hate lying to my family, but we have to keep this between us."

"I didn't lie," he says softly.

I glance over at him.

"Not about that," he clarifies as our eyes connect.

My brows dip, and he squeezes my thigh again with his huge hand.

"Yes, we're lying about the true nature of our relationship and the reasons why you're moving in a little ahead of schedule. In a twisted way, we're *not* lying to the media who *thinks* we're lying. But Jack told me he doesn't want to worry about you. He doesn't want our dynamic on the field to be fucked up because of our personal lives. And it won't. What happens between you and me is between you and me, and that talk with Jack made me realize how important it is that we keep our secret."

I nod. "Agreed." I sigh. "Oh! And I got a call from Dane. He left a voicemail that was a little…concerning."

"What did he say?"

I play the message for him.

"How's he going to get your attention?" he asks.

I shrug. "I have no idea."

"Better let Ellie know just so we can stay ahead of it."

I nod. "Good idea." I forward her the voicemail and cross my fingers Dane doesn't do anything to mess up what we've got going here.

Ellie texts back a minute later.

Ellie: *Hopefully it's just a threat. Let's wait it out.*

We pull into Ben's driveway, and the same photographer that's been posted across the street for the last couple weeks is there again. He snaps our pictures as we unload my boxes. It has to be pretty clear I'm moving in, and Jack's arranging to have all the furniture I ordered for my apartment dropped off tomorrow.

Once my boxes are all inside and up in the guest room to keep up the appearance we're putting on for my family, we set to work on rearranging the minimal furniture at Ben's place to make room for the items coming tomorrow.

"You getting hungry?" Ben asks as I start unpacking my clothes as I make myself at home in the guest room.

I nod.

"I'll start dinner. Just yell down if you need any help."

"Thanks. Yell up if you need any, too, but I won't be much help in the kitchen."

He chuckles. "Don't worry. As long as you can try to carry a tune, I can teach you how to cook."

I tilt my head in a bit of confusion at his comment, but I let it go as I fix my hangers and begin organizing my closet by color—the way it always was, but some of the items were moved out of order during the move.

About a half hour later, Ben appears in my doorway as I'm organizing my underwear drawer. "Dinner's just about ready. And why bother with anything in that drawer when it's just going to end up on the floor anyway?" He flashes me a grin, and I offer a small smile.

His eyes widen with alarm. "What's wrong?"

I shake my head. "Nothing."

He steps into the room and sits on the edge of my bed "Usually you laugh at my stupid jokes."

I sit beside him and fidget with my hands in my lap. "I'm sorry. I just…" I blow out a breath. "I'm worried about what Dane's planning. He's the competitive type, and he doesn't quit until he gets what he wants."

Ben reaches over and covers my hands with one of his. "If you want to be with him, it's okay, Peaches."

"I don't," I say softly. "I thought I did…but I know what I want, and it isn't him." I glance a little timidly over at Ben, and he turns to look at me at the same time. Our eyes connect, and that same heat that's always there between us warms the air around us.

He squeezes my hands. "We'll figure it out together, okay?" he says softly, and then he leans in and presses a soft kiss to my lips.

I nod. "Okay."

"We can't worry about something that we can't control. We can be as proactive as we want, and we can control how we react, but sitting here letting what *might* happen affect our present is just a waste of time."

I blow out a breath. "You're right."

"Now get that cute little ass downstairs before I burn dinner."

I giggle. "Yes, sir."

"Oh sweet Jesus," he says, closing his eyes and stretching his neck back for a second. "Say that again."

"Mm. Yes, sir." I lower my voice and draw out the words on a soft moan.

"Oh, fuck. After dinner, your ass is mine."

"Just my ass? You can have my whole body, Trouble."

He laughs, and I think we're both definitely going to enjoy this new living arrangement.

CHAPTER 29

Ben

"Something smells fantastic," she says as she walks into the kitchen. Two plates are set up on the kitchen counter, and to the top right of each plate sits one small cup like you get at a restaurant for dipping sauce and a little bowl with what looks like salsa in it.

"That's probably either me or Buddy," I deadpan as I pull a tray out of the oven.

She rolls her eyes. "Between those two choices, I definitely think it's Buddy."

I laugh, and the scent she sniffed when she walked into the room gets stronger as I set the tray from the oven on the counter.

"What are we having?" she asks.

"Barbeque chicken with pineapple salsa and cilantro lime rice."

Both her brows rise. "You know how to make that?"

I shrug. "It's not that hard."

"But, like, you *made* it? It's not just a reheat?"

"It's not just a reheat." I nod toward one of the stools at the counter, and she sits. "And it's all homemade. The barbeque sauce is my Gramma Jean's recipe. I came up with the salsa myself after I had something similar at a restaurant."

I grab a piece of chicken off the tray and slide it onto her plate. "And the rice is just a pretty easy, standard recipe." I put some chicken on my plate, too, and then I grab the pot from the stove and scoop a little rice onto each plate.

"It looks delicious," she says. "What's for dessert?"

I raise both brows and lick my lips as I give her the heated look that almost always works on women. "You."

She giggles. "Who knew you had all these hidden talents?"

My brows dip. "Football and cooking?"

She lifts a shoulder. "Don't forget about the sex."

I wiggle my brows and offer a cheeky grin before I toss a cup of food in Buddy's bowl and sit on the stool beside her.

She digs in with her first bite, and she tips her neck back and closes her eyes like she's in ecstasy. The monster definitely wakes up at that.

"Enjoying it?" I ask, and she nods.

"It's fantastic, Ben. And it's kind of incredible how you continue to surprise me."

Surprises seem to be my specialty, I guess.

Or they were, the last time I was in any sort of romantic relationship. Back before I got totally burned by the woman I thought I loved. Back when I saw a completely different future for myself than the road I ultimately started to travel.

We make light conversation through dinner and take Buddy for a long walk after dinner. We hold hands and don't really care whether there's someone following us who has a camera. I stop and kiss her near the park—the midway point of our walk before we turn around to head back home, and when I get her home, I take her up to my bed and show her how deeply my feelings are starting to go.

As I pump into her, every thrust is another sentence I can't say. It's not that I don't feel it—because I do.

Emotion hits me as the monster unleashes his venom right into her pretty little cunt. I don't know if I'll ever be able to say the words to her. Communication is not my strong suit. But as I watch her unravel as her own orgasm plows headfirst into her, I wish I could tell her what I'm feeling.

I am in love with Kaylee. I don't know how or why or when it happened, but it did. Without a doubt.

But for some reason, the words won't form on my tongue.

I pull out of her and collapse beside her, the words in my brain unable to move from there to my mouth.

She snuggles into my side, tossing an arm over my chest. I feel her tits as they settle in against my ribs, and if I didn't just come seconds ago, I'd be ready to go again. That's all it takes. Kaylee's hot tits rubbing against me. Her nipples in my mouth. Her hot, needy cunt as it grips onto my cock and takes everything from me.

I'm falling for you is an understatement. That I can say, but that doesn't really encompass the true heart of what's going on in my chest.

Saying *I love you* is another story entirely.

I love you brings back the feelings of the past. The three small words bring back all the huge emotions I felt when the little secrets Tatum had been keeping from me were finally exposed. Those words are the entire reason why I don't want kids in my own future, and it's not just because of the way I grew up with my mom constantly harping on my dad and then eventually cheating on him. It has a lot more to do with what Tatum did.

I don't allow myself to go there. I don't allow myself to think about it because when I do, it feels as fresh as the day it all happened.

I don't want to see her. I have to, but that doesn't mean I have to like it. If Montana didn't hold such a firm grip on me, the fact that she's still there might be enough to drive me away for good.

But when I think of my place up there, I know I'll never really be able to leave for good. It's my sanctuary. It's the only place that's ever *really* felt like home. It's the place I can escape to when I need some time to myself. It's all the things my normal, day-to-day life isn't, and I deserve that refuge. I know I do, and I won't allow Tatum being in the same state to be the final straw that drives me out.

We fall asleep after we clean up, and when I wake up, it's because someone is licking my hand.

And it isn't Kaylee.

Buddy's ready for a walk.

"Just a second, Buddy," I say softly, and then I shift as slowly as I can so I don't wake her, but I fail. She moans a little as she moves to stretch.

"Morning," she says, her voice sleepy and sexy.

"Morning," I say. "Buddy's ready for a walk. Want to join me?"

"Does Buddy run?" she asks.

I nod. "Buddy does. Ben does not. Not this early, anyway."

She chuckles softly as she sits up. "Ben's going to start. Get your running shoes on, my friend."

I have a meeting with my trainer later today and I'll definitely be paying the price for an extra run later tonight, but her challenge paired with the pleading look on my dog's face convinces me. "Fine. Meet me in the kitchen in ten minutes."

"Make it nine," she says, and one of the things I love about her is her competitive spirit.

Yep. I just said *love*. In my head, of course.

And I find that running isn't such a chore when I get to do it with Kaylee. She makes it fun, even. And as an added bonus, I get to watch her perky ass bounce up and down.

When we get back from our run, we're both breathless and sweaty, so we head out to the backyard to drink water and stretch while Buddy runs around in the grass. It's pure bliss here this morning, and that should've been my first clue that things were off. History has proven that bliss doesn't last very long, and today is certainly no different.

As I'm selecting a new song for our stretch playlist on my phone, a text from Ellie comes through. It's to both Kaylee and me.

Ellie: *Looks like it wasn't just an empty threat. [Link]*

"Shit," I mutter.

Kaylee glances up. "What's wrong?"

"New video," I say. She comes over to watch with me, and I click the link. That goddamn fool Billy Peters pops up.

He snaps his fingers at the camera. "It's a *Celebrity Snaps Oh Snap Preview!*" he says with way too much enthusiasm. "Coming at nine PM Eastern time tonight, check out my one-on-one interview with Dane Parker, ex-boyfriend of sexy Vegas Aces tight end Ben Olson's new *girlfriend*. He's got a ton of tea to spill today and it is *piping* hot." My face splashes across the screen when he says my name, and Kaylee darts across when he mentions the word *girlfriend*, which he finger quotes.

The shot cuts to Kaylee's ex.

"We wanted different things for our future," he says. "She wanted four or five kids, and at the time, I didn't."

The video cuts back to Billy. "She wants kids? Check this out."

A video with *me* in it fills the screen, and it's moments like these that I really fucking hate the digital age in which we live. A freshly fucked woman took on the role of an interviewer after we had sex a couple of years ago. I was drunk while she took video of me and posted it for the world to see.

"So, Benny Boy, are you *ever* going to settle down and commit to just one woman?"

In the video, I shake my head. "Fuck no. No commitment, no marriage, no kids. Not now, not ever. Football is life."

"There you have it, friends," Billy says. The words flash across the screen with my voice repeating them three times. *No commitment, no marriage, no kids.* "Tune in tonight at nine PM Eastern live when I'll have Dane Parker in the studio with me as we play the interview and talk more afterward. See you then!" Billy snaps his fingers and the video ends.

I draw in a deep breath through my nose and exhale through my mouth.

"Shit," Kaylee says, and Buddy saunters over with a little whine, like even he's getting annoyed with this asshole's obsession with my life.

"Come on," I say, nodding toward the house. "Let's go inside and call Ellie." Better to make this call inside rather than in the yard. I dial Ellie and put her on speakerphone.

"Hey," she answers.

"What the fuck is wrong with this guy?" I ask.

"Doesn't matter. We can only control our reaction. You still opposed to a marriage?"

I blow out a breath. Yeah. Still opposed.

"Why do we care?" Kaylee asks. "It's just one guy's opinion."

"For one thing, we care because I don't want your ex doing this shit to you," I say. I try to keep the tenderness I feel for her out of my tone, but I'm pretty sure I fail. "Your relationship with him should have stayed between the two of you and it's bullshit that it isn't."

"What do you think Dane wants?" Ellie asks. "Money? His fifteen minutes of fame?"

"Attention," Kaylee says. "He's a stubborn ass who will stop at nothing to win."

"I know some guys like that," she deadpans. "We have a couple options. We can sit back quietly and wait it out or we can respond. Thoughts?"

"I vote for wait it out," Kaylee says.

"Kay, we can stop him from posting this shit," I say.

She shrugs. "I don't care if he posts it."

"You don't?" Ellie asks. "Even though he's obliterating what we're trying to do in front of the media?"

I nod at Kaylee as I widen my eyes pointedly. The only reason she wouldn't care if he posted it is if we're in a real relationship...which we are, but Ellie can't know that.

Kaylee nods as she gets my secret meaning. "I just meant I don't care what Dane says. I don't want him back," she clarifies weakly, but Ellie buys it.

"Okay. We sit back and let the shit show unfold, but can you two at least be out in public somewhere at nine PM Eastern to make it a little easier on me?" Ellie asks.

"Yeah," I say.

And I know what I need to do. It won't be tonight since I have a little planning I need to do, and the thought of what I'm planning terrifies the ever living fuck out of me, but right now...it feels like my only possible avenue.

CHAPTER 30

Kaylee

It's a little before lunchtime when the doorbell rings and Buddy lets the whole neighborhood know we have a visitor. I open the door to Jeb…which reminds me that he went on a date with my mom two nights ago. I've been so caught up in moving in with Ben and having sex with Ben and running with Ben and fighting the media with Ben and falling in love with Ben that I totally forgot about their date.

"Hi Mr. Olson," I say.

"Please, it's Jeb."

I nod. "Come on in. How was dinner with my mom?"

He chuckles. "No beating around the bush."

I shake my head. "Never. Did you two have fun?"

"We had a nice conversation and that was all."

I narrow my eyes at Ben's dad. "I haven't talked to my mom yet, but I'm going to check to be sure your stories match up."

He laughs as Ben bounds down the stairs, fresh from the shower. His hair is still wet and slicked back a little. He's freshly shaven, and it's sort of incredible how he could look just as hot with or without stubble, with or without wet hair, with or without clothes. Et cetera. He's just fine as hell.

"What do you want, old man?" Ben asks.

"Brunch," Jeb says pointedly.

"Oh shit, I'm sorry." Ben slaps his dad on the back genially. "I totally forgot it's Sunday."

"Brunch?" I ask, raising a brow. "Do you two go out to brunch on Sundays?"

Ben chuckles as he shakes his head. "No. I make us brunch on Sundays. Not *every* Sunday—"

Jeb holds up a hand rather than interrupting Ben's words. "Every Sunday you're not in season."

Ben twists his lips. "That's how it started." He holds up his hands in defense. "But I'm a busy dude."

Busy getting laid.

Okay, to be fair, that's not what we were doing this morning, but I have a feeling it could be why he cancelled previous Sunday brunches with Dad.

I don't want to think about that.

Jeb looks over at me. "It started as a weekly way to check in on the kid while still getting a decent meal. As you might've heard, my mother taught him how to cook, and his food tastes like hers." He shrugs good-naturedly, and every time I talk to him, I like him a little more.

I like how he's playing off wanting to check in on his son as a way to get a good meal. It seems like these two have such a close bond, and it's sweet.

It makes me happy.

It makes me miss my own dad. Fiercely. But a lot of things do. That loss is just something that never goes away. It doesn't get easier, but the fresh slice of pain fades a little with time as you learn to live in a new normal.

Ben looks at his dad and jerks his head toward the kitchen. "Get your ass in there and start cracking eggs."

I giggle and follow the two of them into the kitchen. "Can I help?"

Ben shakes his head. "We've got this."

I perch on one of the stools as I watch the comedy scene unfold.

Jeb is stilted and unnatural in the kitchen with his cowboy boots, jeans, and flannel shirt, this one a combination of light and dark blues. He moves slowly and deliberately while his son flies around him gathering cooking utensils and pulling out frypans.

Ben's graceful, which is amazing given his size and stature. But it's like a game where he's calling the strategies. "Crack six eggs," he tells his dad, setting a bowl in front of him, and Jeb moves toward the fridge to get the carton of eggs.

Meanwhile, Ben gathers a few things from the pantry. Once Jeb is out of the way of the fridge, Ben grabs sausage and bacon. He sets everything on the counter beside the stove then turns toward me. "I do have a job for you."

I nod eagerly, and he hands me two potatoes, a bowl, and a peeler.

"Can you peel those?"

"Sure," I say. I've peeled a few things in my day. Not many, but enough to know how to use a peeler. I'm as slow as Jeb so I don't slice a finger off, shaving off a part of the peel before moving the peeler back to its starting point and shaving off the next peel. When I glance up, I spot Ben tilting his head as he watches me.

"Want to see a cool trick?" he asks.

I shrug, and he walks over to my side of the counter. He takes the peeler and potato from me, and then he proceeds to move the peeler in a back-and-forth motion. "Both sides of the peeler are sharp, so you can peel twice as fast."

I watch as he does the entire potato in about seven seconds flat. It would've taken me ten times longer than him to do that same thing.

"Now you try," he says, nodding toward the second potato. I'm still pretty slow, but it does go much faster to use both sides of the peeler. "Good," he says, and I preen. It's silly, but the compliment in an area where I consider myself a complete failure feels incredible.

When I glance up, he's giving me a look of approval. "You've got potential, kid. I'm going to teach you how to cook."

I look up at him in horror. "What if I don't want to learn?" It's not my forte, but I've also never given it a try, and more importantly, I've never had such a hot teacher. He makes me want to learn.

He laughs. "What do you think we're going to do in Montana all summer?"

"Make dinner?" I guess.

"Bingo!"

I giggle, and I continue watching the Ben and Jeb comedy hour as they work. Ben has me dice two tomatoes after he shows me how, and somehow I manage to do it to his approval.

A half hour later, Ben sets plates on the kitchen table with homemade breakfast burritos piled high with his special salsa recipe.

And it's fantastic.

"Delicious," Jeb says, his only compliment on the meal, while I rave on and on about how good it is and practically climax right at the table when a crisp potato mixes with a little shot of perfectly cooked bacon.

"I'm in for weekly Sunday brunch," I say with a grin.

"You sticking around a while?" Jeb asks.

Ben fields that one with a smile. "She's sticking around a while."

Jeb nods once. "Good."

That's all he says, but the way he says it and the underlying meaning from a man of relatively few words means a lot.

I call my mom once he heads home to get the *real* story about their date. "How was dinner on Friday?" I ask once she answers.

She laughs. "Getting right to the point I see."

"Well?"

"It was nice. It wasn't romantic, so get that idea out of your head."

"But could it be?" I press, mostly because I still don't want my mom doing my boyfriend's dad.

"It's early for all that, honey," she says gently.

"I just had brunch with him."

"You did?" she asks. And then she can't help herself. "What did he say?"

I knew it. I knew she was interested in something romantic with him.

Ew.

I mean, yay for her, but ew.

"He said you two had a nice conversation."

"We did," she affirms.

"He talks?" I ask.

She laughs. "Not too much about himself, but once you get him going on his son, he doesn't stop."

I get it. Ben is the type of guy a person could rave about for hours.

We wrap up our call with little else in the way of details, and then I make sure I have everything in place for school this week. I check in on my Instagram account and check my email, and I find a few from Kate and a few from Ellie. Kate's have the social proof calculations, and Ellie sends me a few new sponsorship contracts, of which I sign two new ones.

Nine PM Eastern inches closer and closer, and I get more and more nervous as the day goes on.

It's half past five when a text from Dane comes through.

Dane: *You have the power to stop this.*

In a half hour, we'll all get to see what questions Billy asked him and how he answered.

But instead of obsessing about it, we're going out. Ben is taking me to dinner and then to one of his favorite nightclubs for drinks afterward.

When Billy Peters' audience tunes in tonight as his interview with my ex goes live, he won't be able to count Ben and me among his loyal following.

I don't even bother with a reply, in part because I don't want to, but also because we're leaving in a few minutes for dinner.

"You look hot," he says when I walk into the kitchen.

I laugh. "Thank you. So do you."

He pulls me into his arms. "We could skip all this and just go get naked."

"We could," I murmur against his lips. "But that would be doing the opposite of what Ellie requested of us."

"Who cares?" he says, his lips against my neck as I lean back to give him more room.

I sigh, and he pauses then pulls back.

"You okay?"

I lift a shoulder. "Not really. I want to know what he says."

"Babe, you have got to chill. People say shit all the time. It's the nature of the business and it's the nature of being with someone in my position. I will always have haters and as long as you're with me, you will too."

I nod. "I know. I've seen it firsthand. It's just never been about *me* before."

He rubs his hands gently up and down my back. "Let's go out and have some fun. Let's not worry about the interview until we get home. Then we can watch it, tear it apart, and have Ellie figure out any damage control we need. Sound good?"

It sounds perfect, actually…even though the thought that he knew exactly what to do to quell my yelling brain is more than a little terrifying considering the end date stamped across our union.

CHAPTER 31

Ben

I only get her a *little* drunk. She does, after all, have to show up at a job tomorrow where she has to be a professional in front of a classroom with thirty-some-odd students in it.

We each have a couple drinks at dinner, and we're seated in the center of the restaurant (one with good lighting, naturally) to allow anyone who wants to snap our photo to do it. I see the funny angles of phones from across the room as people take their shots. They think they're being covert. They're not.

But that's sort of the point of why we're here.

And to be honest, I've never shied away from it anyway. Being the center of attention is part of my brand at this point. You don't get labeled *The Big O* and you can't be known for your *Big O Thunder* if you expect to sit shyly in a corner.

It's an early dinner, but the point is to be out in public when the video premieres. The point is to show that we're united and whatever tricks other people have up their sleeves isn't going to affect the two of us.

The ironic part of all of this is that we actually *are* a couple, and instead of tearing us apart like they're trying to do, they just keep pushing us together.

Would it be easier to just admit the truth to everyone?

Of course it would.

But it's not what either of us wants right now. We just want to have fun with the time we have together because once the contract ends, we don't know what will happen.

Maybe we'll stay together.

Maybe one of us will run scared at the end, and maybe one of us will run scared long before the expiration date.

I can't think that far ahead. Instead, I intend to live in the here and now.

It's funny how I can be affectionate with her in public but not in private when I'm with her family, but I take full advantage of leaning over to kiss her before our plates are set in front of us or resting my paw on her thigh or tossing an arm over the back of her chair.

All of it feels good. Natural. Like I want to keep doing it.

We head to the club after dinner. It's still early, but a few people are around. We sit at the bar and have a couple drinks—publicly, of course, so someone somewhere catches a photo of us. And after we're both at a point where we're starting to get tipsy, I nod toward the hostess. This is one of my buddy Mike's clubs, which means not only are drinks on the house, but so is the private VIP suite the hostess leads us to.

Once we both have fresh, full drinks in hand, the hostess leads us to a dark hallway along the back wall, and we climb the stairs to the suite level. There are six suites here, and she leads us to one in the middle. "This one has the best view," she says, and she unlocks the door and lets us in.

There's a huge windowed wall overlooking the dance floor on the opposite side of the room from where we stand. "It's a two-way mirror," the hostess says, and she leads us over to the wall. We walk through the room which has a counter along the wall we came in on one side of the door and a private bathroom on the other side. Couches are in the center of the room, and the couches point to the window wall to overlook the dance floor below.

She opens a door in the wall I hadn't even noticed, and it leads out to a small balcony we can stand on to overlook the crowd below. The balcony is a tight fit, and it strikes me as strange that granite top pub table and four chairs tucked tightly into it sits right outside the door. There's barely enough clearance for the door to swing open all the way, but if the table was a few feet over to one side, the chairs would get in the way of actually being able to walk out onto the balcony.

The dance floor started filling up with people since we arrived about an hour ago, and this is a great vantage point to dance by ourselves or people watch (or get drunk and fuck on the couch, which is my current preference).

The hostess leaves a bottle of vodka on the table—Kaylee's current drink preference—along with a bucket of beer for me, and we each take a seat at the table on the small balcony with our drinks.

Someone down on the floor recognizes me up here even in the dark. I blame all the sponsorships. My face is fucking everywhere these days, and a smattering of people start waving. Some whip out phones to take photos exactly as we wanted so the world knows we were out together tonight and we don't care about her ex's interview. I grin at the fans I wave back down to, but the truth is that I just want a few minutes alone with Kaylee.

When I look over at her and catch her eye, I find that she's giving me *the look*. You know—the one where she's saying *fuck me now*. And who am I to deny what she wants?

We abandon our drinks on the table as I take her hand then guide her inside. She closes the door behind us.

The two-way mirrored doors allow us to look out over the clubgoers perched high above them without being seen ourselves, and even better…I can slam Kaylee's sweet little ass against the glass and nobody will be the wiser. I'm definitely thinking *this* is where we should fuck rather than the couch.

I back her up against the wall and I shove my tongue down her throat.

It's hot.

We start kissing like we did that first night I finger fucked her under her brother's dining room table—when I got her up to her bedroom and I grabbed her throat and we kissed like our lives depended on it.

That's this kiss, too. It's urgent and needy and it's taking me to a place beyond horniness. But it's still a little different.

It's her and me now. We've teamed up against the world as we take on the media frenzy, but we're also holding this secret of ours, and there's something special about that.

I'm a *little* drunk, too, I guess, but I'm out with my girlfriend so it's not a big deal. It's not like we're going to hit the media. I reach under the bottom of her dress and push it up enough to give myself access. She moans into me, and I thrust my rock hard cock against her as I try to take it slow.

I don't want to take it slow.

I want to shove my fat cock into her pretty little cunt.

I've always enjoyed sex, obviously. But with her, it's different. I don't just *enjoy* it. I crave it. Constantly.

When I'm not inside her, I'm thinking about being inside her.

And when I am inside her, I feel like I'm home. It's this intrinsic feeling I've never felt before that crushes my chest in the kind of way I never want to stop feeling.

I'm terrified of it.

I'm addicted to it.

I'm addicted to *her*.

The booze and the clubs and the strippers and the random sex with strangers is all fun and has a time and place. But the more time I spend with her, the more that time and place feels cemented into my past. It's not my future.

She is.

I inch my way up her leg to get closer to her pussy, and she shifts to allow me a little easier access. I slip her panties to the side and immediately find out how fucking drenched she is as she waits for this with as much anticipation as me.

She tilts her head back against the wall as I shove two fingers up into her, and that's when it happens. The door in the mirrored wall—the one we somehow shifted and didn't realize we were leaning on—flies open.

It all happens so quickly that I don't even realize what's going on at first. I somehow manage to pull my hand from under her skirt and clutch her a tightly to me as she starts to fall backward and I start to fall on top of her.

It seems like it's all happening in slow motion.

I do what I can to protect her, but when she goes down, she slams her head on the hard granite surface of the table. She yells out in pain as her eyes squeeze shut tightly.

"Fuck!" I yell. I shift to the side so I don't fall on top of her, and that's when the side of my body crashes into the table, too. My eyes are on Kaylee, whose body seems to have gone limp, as our drinks go flying and the bottle of vodka the hostess left behind tips over the railing of the balcony.

A story below us, people are dancing and having a great time as a vodka bottle falls from the sky.

I yell out a warning, but the music is too loud.

Nobody hears me.

A sharp pain slices through my body, but I'm more concerned about Kaylee than myself. I get crashed into every Sunday with worse than this.

Okay, maybe not *worse* than a granite countertop.

It takes me a half second to get my bearings, and when I do, I spot Kaylee. She's still on the ground, and she isn't moving.

I leap up despite the pain pulsing from my chest through to my back, and I grab her into my arms with a fresh, sharp burn slicing through me as I move her to the couch in the suite, my leg pushing off the table while I get us the fuck off the balcony.

"Kaylee!" I yell. "Wake up! Kaylee!" *Come on, Peaches. Open your eyes.* "Kaylee! Somebody help!" I yell, but nobody hears me. I can't just leave her, but I need to get her help. I need her to open her eyes. "Help!"

I need her to be okay.

Fear plows into me.

Fear for her safety and wellness.

Fear for the people below us.

Fear for my own body and the pain that continues to pulse along with the consequences of what just happened and whether either will be bad enough to affect the future of my career.

But above all that, one fear pulses the loudest, and it's somehow the most terrifying of all.

It's the fear that this one event will change the course of the relationship I've started building with the woman I've fallen in love with.

The woman who is currently lying unresponsive on a couch in a nightclub after hitting her head.

To be continued in book 3, TIGHT FIT.

ACKNOWLEDGMENTS

I'll save my acknowledgments for the final book since I know you're ready to get to *Tight Fit*... and I can't wait for you to see what's next.

xoxo,
Lisa Suzanne

ABOUT THE AUTHOR

Lisa Suzanne is a romance author who resides in Arizona with her husband and two kids. She's a former high school English teacher and college composition instructor. When she's not cuddling or chasing her kids, she can be found working on her latest book or watching reruns of *Friends*.

ALSO BY LISA SUZANNE

HOME GAME
Vegas Aces Book One
#1 Bestselling Sports Romance

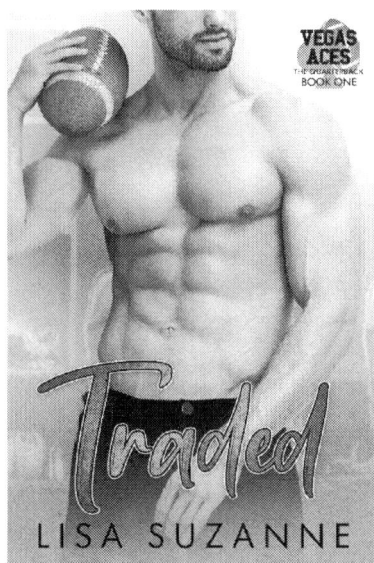

Traded
Vegas Aces: The Quarterback Book One
#1 Bestselling Football Romance

Printed in Great Britain
by Amazon